"It wasn't supposed ⟨to be a trick⟩ question," Claire sa⟨id.⟩

"I just meant what are your hobbies? What do you do in your spare time when you're not preaching or leading youth group?"

A teasing smile lit up her face and his breath stumbled in a way he hadn't expected.

"Wait, let me guess." She settled back in the chair, making herself comfortable like she intended to stay a good long while.

She tilted her head to one side. "In high school, you were a jock."

Sam shook his head slowly back and forth. "You could not be more wrong."

"Oh? Tell me more."

Sam knew what she was doing. Claire Casey was not the type of person who wanted to leave a room feeling dismissed. Because he had tried to cut their conversation short, she would do everything she could to make it last, just to prove a point.

Something about the way she gazed at him made Sam afraid he was suddenly going to spill all of his secrets.

Donna Gartshore loves reading and writing. She also writes short stories, poetry and devotionals. She often veers off to the book section in the grocery store when she should be buying food. Besides talking about books and writing, Donna loves spending time with her daughter, Sunday family suppers and engaging online with the writing community.

Books by Donna Gartshore

Love Inspired

Instant Family
Instant Father
Finding Her Voice
Finding Their Christmas Home
A Secret Between Them
The Courage to Love

Visit the Author Profile page at LoveInspired.com.

THE COURAGE TO LOVE

DONNA GARTSHORE

LOVE INSPIRED
INSPIRATIONAL ROMANCE

LOVE INSPIRED®
INSPIRATIONAL ROMANCE

ISBN-13: 978-1-335-93699-8

The Courage to Love

Copyright © 2024 by Donna Lynn Gartshore

Love Inspired
22 Adelaide St. West, 41st Floor
Toronto, Ontario M5H 4E3, Canada
www.LoveInspired.com

Printed in Lithuania

Recycling programs for this product may not exist in your area.

MIX
Paper | Supporting responsible forestry
FSC® C021394

And the Lord, he it is that doth go before thee;
he will be with thee, he will not fail thee,
neither forsake thee: fear not, neither be dismayed.
—*Deuteronomy* 31:8

For my daughter, as always.

My mom and sisters, who always cheer me on.

My writing friends, who always inspire me
with their unique talent.

For all people who face life with courage and
determination, though they may be struggling with
things we know nothing about.

And for God, who knows everything
and endlessly loves us.

Chapter One

Claire Casey was rummaging in her purse to find the keys to lock up Love Blooms, the flower shop she owned in the small town of Living Skies, Saskatchewan, when she heard her cell phone ringing.

It was the middle of November, already getting dark out by the time she closed the shop, and the air was frosty.

She immediately abandoned the search for her keys and rummaged for her phone instead, praying that it wasn't something urgent with her four-year-old daughter, Maggie.

Juggling being a twenty-eight-year-old single mother with being the business owner of a shop she hoped to expand was a challenge every day, and Claire was grateful that her sister, Rachel, who shared their apartment-style condo, was able to step in to do day-care pickups on the days Claire was running late at work and keep Maggie entertained until Claire got home.

Even though Rachel was home some of the time, Maggie still went to day care because Claire thought it was good for her to interact with other children and because Rachel needed time to look for work.

Her gratitude was tinged with guilt, because while she was grateful for Rachel's current availability, she wasn't glad of the reason. Rachel was currently unemployed. She was a talented artist but it was difficult to find full-time work in the arts.

Claire knew there had been a lot of speculating when she got pregnant and especially when she chose to keep Maggie and raise her on her own. There had also been surprise, because until then, Claire was never one to want to make waves or draw attention to herself. Her parents made it clear that they weren't pleased with her taking this stand, although there wasn't any doubt now that they adored their granddaughter.

All Claire could say was that being a Christian didn't exempt anyone from being human and making bad choices, but she never thought of Maggie as a mistake. She loved her daughter and wanted to give her the world.

All of this ran through her head as she fumbled to answer her phone as quickly as possible. But the voice that said "Oh, Claire, I'm so glad I caught you" wasn't Rachel's. It belonged to Shirley Allen, a popular Realtor in town and a member of the book club Claire belonged to.

"Hi, Shirley, what's going on?"

"Would you be able to pick Troy up from school and drop him off for youth group at the church?" Shirley asked, referring to her fourteen-year-old son, who was a freshman at Living Skies High School. "He stayed after school for basketball practice. I have to meet clients over an issue that's come up at the house they've been looking at, and Bernie is away on another business trip. I've tried everyone I can think of and you're the first one I've been able to reach. I'm so sorry. I know you must be anxious to get home to that little girl of yours. It wouldn't normally be a bad walk for Troy, but he'll have all his equipment and books with him, and all of this melting and freezing has made things a little icy."

"It's absolutely no trouble," Claire assured her. "I'd be happy to give Troy a ride. I'll give my sister a call and let her know."

She didn't mention that she hoped she wouldn't run into the assistant pastor, Samuel Meyer. She had no complaints about his sermons when he was filling in for the main pastor, Liam Barker, at Good Shepherd Church. He was a dynamic, passionate and articulate speaker and there was no doubt that the youth group was flourishing under his leadership. But they had sat in the same town-council meetings, and for whatever reason, if she said something was black, Sam Meyer insisted that it was white. They just couldn't see eye to eye on anything. He was especially dismissive of her wish to expand her flower shop and had made it abundantly clear that he thought the space could be put to better use.

But Claire knew what her own reasons were and she wasn't about to be swayed from them. Not only did she want to be in the financial position to ensure that none of Maggie's needs went unmet, she also considered flower arranging to be how she expressed herself creatively, and being creative meant so much to her, as it was a significant way that she honored the Creator.

In reality, Claire was aware she wasn't in a position to push for the property when she didn't yet have the funds to accommodate any significant changes, but she imagined a future where she could hire employees and have more time to spend with Maggie. Maybe Rachel could be one of those employees and put her talents to use to give the shop an artistic flair.

Claire had never relished looking to others for support. Her independent streak started when she was never part of a large and loyal group of friends at school, and was cemented by Maggie's father taking off and by her parents making it clear they had no intentions of rescuing her from the burdens she would face as a single mother. She did not want to be obligated to a bank or anyone else for the funds, so she was saving as best she could.

She had been diligent in doing so and was getting so close to having the money she would need for a down payment. Putting up a fight for the property was her way of telling herself that she believed it would work out. She trusted that God was in on the plan.

Now, if only Pastor Sam would quit standing in the way. It disturbed her more than she wanted to admit that he was so dismissive of why she needed the flower shop.

But now was not the time to dwell on that and she made herself listen to Shirley.

"You're the absolute best," Shirley said. "I'll text Troy and let him know to expect you and that I'll pick him up from youth group. Thanks a million."

"No problem. Happy to help." Claire hung up, found her keys and locked up, then went to her car, which was parked behind the shop.

She walked carefully since, as Shirley had mentioned, the sidewalks were slick.

Before starting the car, she gave her sister a quick call and explained the situation.

"No problem," Rachel said. "We've been making our Christmas wish lists and I'll get supper started soon."

Claire didn't ask if employment was on Rachel's list.

There were times when Claire allowed herself to wonder what it would be like to have a husband and a full-time father for her daughter. But Maggie's biological father hadn't been responsible enough to fit the bill and she wasn't going to bring a man into their lives just for the sake of having one, regardless of what others may think. Maybe that made her a bit closed off, even a bit hard at times, but that whole ordeal had taught her to protect her own heart, and now she had a little girl's heart to protect, too.

Meanwhile, she would focus on what God had provided for them and set goals to create a fulfilling future for herself and for Maggie.

As she often did, Claire let her imagination loose, picturing what an expanded flower shop could mean to them. She visualized a large, bright room, teeming with customers being helped by friendly and knowledgeable staff. Rachel's artistic talent would enhance the beauty of all of the bouquets—maybe she could design her own cards and sell them there.

Claire also imagined a small section of devotionals in the shop, along with stationery and whimsical knickknacks.

Claire arrived at the high school and saw that the parking lot was jammed with cars, so she parked on the street a little ways away and headed toward the school. Students and some parents were milling about, the teens shouting things back and forth.

As she was walking across the parking lot, a snowball was hurled in her general direction and a youth came from her blind side, colliding into her as he twisted his body to avoid the hit.

"Watch it, fatso," the boy said before darting off.

Claire's heart froze like the ground below, preventing her from calling after the boy to demand an apology for his smashing into her. She breathed slowly, in and out, and prayed to remember that she was beautiful in the Lord's sight, and that the boy who had so thoughtlessly insulted her was simply an immature youth who lacked guidance.

Claire had struggled with her weight for as long as she could remember, and in school there had been some taunts because of it, but with a lot of prayer and focus on the positive attributes she believed God had given her, she had learned not to let her size define her. She took care of her appearance, loved experimenting with hairstyles and makeup, and had developed a knack for choosing clothes that were stylish and colorful, bringing out the luster in her almost black hair and the shine in her aqua eyes.

Rachel, who was slim herself, had encouraged her and said, "It really bothers me when large women dress like they're trying to hide themselves. You are a beautiful woman, Claire, and you deserve to show it."

Claire also enjoyed regular exercise. No longer using the excuse that she wasn't the athletic type, nothing in her recent life had surprised her more than realizing how much she actually enjoyed biking and walking when weather permitted. Lately, she had attended a variety of exercise classes at the local fitness center. The first time she had set foot into a class, she had held her breath and wrapped her arms around herself in a futile attempt to make herself invisible. But the motivation of the instructors, as well as seeing the variety of ages, shapes and sizes of other participants, soon helped her to relax and be proud of herself for taking the step.

So for the most part, she had come a long way from being the girl who had lamented throughout her school years that she would never be traditionally beautiful or sought after. But there were still setbacks that could momentarily devastate her.

But that was something that she and the Lord would have to hash out later. Claire pulled her attention back to the task at hand and scanned the now thinning crowd to find Troy. She spotted him—a tall, gangly boy—then called out his name and waved.

Shoulders sloping, eyes on the pavement, he ambled toward her. It struck Claire that he wasn't surrounded by jostling, yammering friends, but maybe they'd just left while she was distracted by the rude boy who had smashed into her.

Troy put his things in her back seat and got into the front, buckling up his seat belt without being reminded.

"Your mom messaged that she'll pick you up from youth group?" Claire asked.

He gave a brief nod.

"So how's everything going?" Claire asked after a few seconds of silence. She didn't like the approach of drilling kids about their days, but didn't want to be unfriendly, either.

"S'okay," Troy mumbled in a monotone.

Okay, so clearly he wasn't in a talkative mood. Claire wondered if there was something wrong but, then again, teenage boys weren't exactly her area of expertise. Still, something about his posture and solitariness as he walked toward her car niggled at her. Maybe she could find a way to tactfully talk to Shirley, not to alarm her, but to make sure everything was good with Troy.

There was no more conversation exchanged for the remainder of the drive, so Claire was relieved that it was a short one. She pulled into the church parking lot, turned off the engine and got out.

"I'm good from here," Troy said.

"I'll help you carry your things in," Claire said, opening the back door and gathering his textbooks and notebooks, while he tussled with his gym bag.

She noticed that Troy lengthened his strides, making sure to keep a few steps ahead of her, which amused her, though she held her breath for a moment when his foot skidded on an icy patch. Clearly, he didn't want to be seen with her by any of his friends.

Good Shepherd Church was the church Claire attended, although it wasn't the church she had been raised in and she suspected that her leaving her childhood church still hurt her parents' feelings. But she loved the worship and praise music at Good Shepherd, as well as the Bible studies offered there.

As she juggled Troy's books and followed him down the long corridor to the fellowship room, where the youth group held their gatherings, she heard the unmistakable timbre of Pastor Sam Meyer's voice and she inwardly braced herself.

Troy stopped suddenly and turned. "Okay, we're here," he said, grabbing his books from her in a rather unceremonious manner. "Thanks for the ride," he added hastily, as if he could hear his mother's voice in his head prompting him.

"You're welcome, Troy," Claire said. "Enjoy your evening." She had just turned to walk away when a boy who looked about the same age as Troy burst out of the room, with Sam close behind him.

Every time she saw Sam, she immediately and regretfully registered that she found him more attractive than she wanted to find a man with whom she constantly clashed wills.

He wasn't much taller than her height of five-nine, but he had a comforting solidity about him and carried himself in a way that made him seem taller. His light brown hair was always cut short, combating its tendency to curl, and his hazel eyes could change from probing to gentle in a split second.

He was not classically handsome, by any means—his expression was often serious. But when he did smile it brought a light to his whole face and made Claire want to get to know him better, until she reminded herself that they didn't get along at all, and she detested the way he made her second-guess her own motivations every time he ever-so-calmly pointed out how the property beside her shop could benefit the larger community.

She waited for him to question what she was doing there, even as it struck her as funny, in a kind of pathetic way, that she was already prepared to argue with him.

But as it turned out, he was completely oblivious to her presence, which stung a little, although she didn't know exactly why.

She didn't recognize the boy who had stormed out and assumed that he must be from another high school, possibly one from a nearby town. To his credit, Sam Meyer's youth group had a reputation for being fun, thought-provoking and a safe place for the local youth to explore and share their faith.

But with his face contorted in agitation and his shoulders hunched, the boy seemed to be having the opposite of fun.

"Jason," Sam said, his eyes etched with lines of concern. "What's wrong?"

Jason threw him a baleful look.

Sam raised his hands in a befuddled gesture. "I seriously don't know," he said. "Even though I was in the room, I didn't see or hear anything, but obviously something has upset you. Can you tell me what it was?"

The boy jammed his hands in his pockets and shook his head.

Claire noticed that Troy was mirroring the hands-in-pockets, shoulders-slumped posture, and if not for the fact that the other boy was clearly troubled, she might have dismissed it as teenage boy who was going through a phase.

Which made her wonder again if there was more to Troy's sullenness.

She knew that she should just leave, since it was none of her business, but she couldn't make herself do it. For whatever reason, she had never been good at walking away from a problem.

She was also a little too curious to see how her nemesis, Pastor Sam Meyer, would handle whatever was going on.

It had not been a good day, Sam thought, and apparently it wasn't in God's plans to make it any better.

Then he corrected himself. All days came with a variety of events and he did his best not to label them good or bad. Because for someone who coped with depression the way he did, it was all too easy for the labels to fall on the bad side.

He knew that wasn't something that people who weren't plagued with depression could readily understand. As a matter of fact, people who did suffer from it could vary greatly in how the symptoms manifested themselves.

To start with, he would have to say that he could happily get through a day without the morning phone call with his widowed mother. Oh, he loved his mother and couldn't help but admire her. Hilary Meyer was always a force to be reckoned with. Widow of Clarence Meyer, the former esteemed leader of one of the largest churches in Vancouver, British Columbia, she was a whirlwind of activity and accomplishment—leading women's Bible studies, singing solos in the choir, heading up charitable groups and community activities, serving on every conceivable board. The list seemed endless.

All of this made Sam's role as assistant pastor, at age thirty, at a small-town church somewhat less than impressive, at least by the standards he had grown up with. His mother reminded him of this, in her ever-so-tactful way, almost every time they talked.

His mother was not the kind of person to whom he could explain how his depression made clinging to his faith difficult. She wasn't the kind of person who believed that depression was anything other than something that some self-discipline and a brisk walk could cure.

The truth was that his struggles weren't something that Sam really discussed with anyone. Who needed to know that it was a constant battle for their pastor to face each day? That he believed the Bible was true by sheer will and years of study, and not because he could honestly say that he carried the joy of the Lord in his heart.

Who would want him to teach their children or listen to the occasional sermons he delivered when the head pastor was unavailable, if they knew that the disease he battled often made every word he spoke feel like a lie?

It was difficult to keep up the facade of unquestioning faith in a small town like Living Skies, where he imagined that everyone, let alone a pastor, felt like they were under some scrutiny.

So he had made it a goal to receive a call from a larger church, not only to please his mother, but also because he hoped he might find some release in burying himself in busyness and greater demands...in a place where he might be able to keep people from getting close enough to ask too many questions.

In the meantime, however, he did genuinely care about the kids who attended the youth group. He found their questions, their almost brutal honesty, even their doubts, invigorating. He wanted to help each and every one of them to recognize and grow into their full potential. He was especially grateful for anything that pulled his thoughts out of the gray sludge they often struggled to escape from.

So for two hours every Wednesday night, he ignored the fact that he probably had more struggles with his beliefs than any of them.

His day had begun with yet another reminder that his goal to pastor at a large church was still far out of reach, and was now ending with a teenager who had stormed out of youth group, for reasons he was still trying to figure out, and who was now grimacing at his phone. Then, to top it all off, Claire Casey was standing about a foot away from them, trying to feign disinterest and failing.

He guessed she had given Troy a ride. He knew that Claire was friends with his mother, but that didn't explain why she was still there. Or what it was about her that always made his senses go on high alert.

Sometimes, and he couldn't explain why, he had a sense that she knew he was hiding something. She had a way of studying him across the table at the town-council meetings, with an expression that was solemn and thoughtful…and worse than if it had been openly critical.

Here he was with a puzzle to unravel, but without even trying—or wanting to—he registered that she was wearing her almost black hair up in a messy bun, her red coat brought a flattering glow to her cheeks and she smelled fresh and flowery, as if her skin was naturally scented by the flowers that she sold.

But he had no idea what to do with any of these thoughts. It wasn't like he was about to pursue a serious relationship with a woman whom he could hardly be in the same room as without an argument brewing up between them. In fact, with his struggle to get his life and career on a track that he wanted, he wasn't eager to pursue a serious relationship with anyone. There was no doubt that Claire was an attractive woman with those aqua eyes and glossy dark hair, but her stubbornness in the whole property thing and that way she had of looking at him grated on his nerves.

"Is there something I can help you with, Claire?" Sam

asked, in his shaking-hands-after-church voice, which made her grin, once again giving him the uncomfortable feeling that he couldn't get anything past her.

"I gave Troy a ride," she said, with her tone implying that she had every right to be there. She did, of course, which only made him more frustrated with the situation.

"I see that, and here he is. As you can see, I've got a bit of an issue here…" Wasn't it enough that he had to deal with her constantly challenging him at the town meetings? Could he not get a reprieve from her here at church?

"Okay…" She darted a meaningful look between him and the two boys. Troy was now on his phone.

"Okay?" Sam repeated. His fixed smile made his face feel like hardened clay about to break.

Claire narrowed her eyes and indicated with a head tilt that they should step away for a private conversation. About the last thing he needed was to stand in even closer proximity to her. He had a hard enough time keeping his focus on the matter at hand when she was around. He really didn't enjoy their bickering at meetings and being so unmovable in his stance. But he wanted something more for that vacant space than just flowers. If he could just get Claire to think about the bigger picture, surely she would see he wanted to accomplish something good.

Many churches were sponsoring refugee families from war-torn countries or countries with political strife. But what happened to these families once they were settled? Sam wondered. Yes, there were some follow-up visits and some assistance in finding doctors and dentists, getting the children settled in school and so on. But his heart ached for their fear and loneliness, knowing they'd had to leave behind everything that was familiar to them and, undoubtedly, many loved ones as well.

He had a dream of creating a space where they could gather, reinforce their own community bonds, while also becoming part of their new community: a place where they could continue to learn, not just how to take a bus or fill out a job application, but learn that life could be filled with endless potential.

So, the property wouldn't just be for the newcomers, although they would be the valued center of things, but would be open to all who were willing to share, teach and dream, and become a diverse community together.

To his way of thinking, it would actually be a perfect fit with the popular Wednesday-night classes that were currently offered at the church. Volunteers would offer their skills to do everything from lead a Bible study to encourage the class through preparing a gourmet meal. These classes had, in fact, become so popular that the attendance was rapidly exceeding the space available at Good Shepherd, and what could be better, Sam thought, than to gather old friends and newcomers who could become friends and putting them in an environment to socialize and learn from each other?

But he also wanted it known that it wasn't his goal simply to echo what the church was already doing, or limited to those who all believed the same thing. His vision was for an open-minded, openhearted safe space.

Also, although he was always quick to tell himself it was far from being the only or most important reason, some of the larger churches he had applied to had expressed some interest, but had also indicated that he needed to be able to give some examples of larger projects he'd been involved in, so that they could be assured he was capable of leading a church of their size and scope. He had to forge ahead. He simply could not let them know that his depression made him question his abilities to lead on a daily basis.

All he wanted now, though, was to attempt to salvage what remained of his day.

But it was clear that Claire had no intention of going anywhere until she'd had her say, which was so typical of her, so he told Troy and Jason, "Sorry, guys, I'll just be another minute." He followed Claire a few steps away, looking anxiously over his shoulder at Jason, who was shifting from one foot to the other in an agitated manner.

"I suggest you talk fast," Sam said under his breath. "I could have a mutiny on my hands soon."

"I'll get right to the point, then," Claire said. "I think someone posted something online that upset Jason."

"What do you mean?"

And why are you getting involved in something that doesn't concern you?

Sam grimaced and scratched the side of his face.

"Online. You know…social media, the thing that too many people are addicted to these days."

Sam didn't point out that he had seen her advertisements for Love Blooms on social media, mostly because he wasn't about to admit that he'd been looking.

"Look at them," she persisted.

Sam looked, only because he knew Claire would persist until he did, and could see the way tension radiated from Jason as his eyes flicked over whatever was on his screen, shoulders hunched and mouth set in a rigid line.

"All the kids look at their phones," Sam said, reluctant to admit that Claire had a point, even though he could clearly see the boys weren't happy with what they were reading. "Which is why I usually suggest they try to put them away during group. Troy's looking at his phone as we speak." A troubled expression crossed Claire's face, as if she wanted to add something about that, but then decided not to.

He wasn't going to push her on what it might be. He just wanted her to go away. He counted on familiar routines and ways of doing things to help combat the inner battle about his own worthiness to teach, and having his nemesis hovering around definitely wasn't helping.

"That's true," Claire said. "But Jason is obviously upset. I suggest you get him away from the others and try to find out if he's the victim of online bullying."

"So…you think I can ask him something like that," Sam said slowly, "and he'll just up and spill his heart out to me?"

He shook his head. This woman really didn't get it.

Except…sometimes he was afraid that she did.

Claire's striking aqua eyes widened and her arms folded into a pose he recognized all too well.

He sighed. Why was it that whenever he was around her he always acted in a way he wasn't proud of?

"I do understand what you're saying," he said. "And I think it's great that you're so concerned." He hoped that she could accept that; he wasn't just brushing her off with empty words. "But," he added, "I've been dealing with youth and counseling people for quite a few years now and I've found that approaching people in such a direct manner often just scares them away."

"You mean like not dealing with the problem at all might do?" Claire's mouth, which was so wide and lush when she smiled, had narrowed into a straight line as she nodded toward where Troy now stood by himself.

"Oh, this is not good," Sam groaned, pounding his fist on his chin. "Troy," he said as he strode toward the boy, who looked about as comfortable now as someone who'd been unceremoniously dumped onto another planet with no guarantee that the aliens were friendly. "Did Jason say where he was going?"

"I think he called his mom to come get him."

Now other kids had started to spill out of the room, wondering what was going on. Sam found himself scanning their faces to see if he could pinpoint who might be the type to post something that would hurt Jason. Then he gave his head a quick shake. He was frustrated at himself for allowing Claire to get in his head. He should have been firmer about insisting she leave, church open door policy or not. He had a group to lead and she wasn't part of it.

Although, mostly, the more he thought about it, he was afraid she might have a point, and that irritated him more than anything. But even if it was true that someone had said something hurtful, there was nothing to say it was anyone in the youth group. He just couldn't see that mean-spiritedness in any of them.

Or maybe he just didn't want to.

Dear God, please tell me what I should do.

Then he noticed that a group of the girls were clustered around Claire, whose vivaciousness and sparkling smile made him think that she must save being ornery for him. They were asking her eager questions about her shade of nail polish and where she'd bought her earrings, jolly snowmen that dangled from her ears.

It was just one other way that he and Claire were so different: she was outgoing and exuberant while he, away from the pulpit or youth group, was mostly reserved. It wasn't that he didn't care about people, but it took such energy, sometimes all he had, to battle down the constant barrage of thoughts—the thoughts he knew weren't from God—that he wasn't good enough and that he would never be able to make any real difference.

Sam knew how his depression impacted him. He also knew that others could be so badly affected by despondency that they literally couldn't get out of bed in the morning. He credited his faith, ongoing counseling and medication, which all combined to help him cope as well as he did. He knew and could accept, on some level, that depression was a disease like any other, and that society was finally working together to try to remove its stigma. But society had a long way to go and he still found himself unwilling to share much about his own struggle with it.

All of this didn't make it easy for him to fulfill his mother's wish of him marrying and one day making her a grandmother.

At first, he had been busy getting educated and trying to make his mark in the church, while keeping what he was sure others would consider the liability of his depression under wraps. Now he simply didn't think it would be fair to any woman when he had his own issues to deal with.

If and when he ever did get married, he assumed it would be to someone like his mother—who was quiet, elegant and organized—and certainly not to someone like Claire, whose unrestrained laughter filled the hallway. Sure, he could acknowledge on some level that she was attractive, but she definitely was not his type.

He checked the time. The boys were busy now with their own conversation and he was relieved to see that Troy had joined them. He preferred a much more organized evening, but he tried to press down on his unease by telling himself that it wasn't the end of the world for the kids to go with the flow, as long as they were together and having fun.

Once again, Claire's suggestion about what might have happened came back to trouble him. He just didn't know what he was going to do about it. Maybe the next time the teens gathered together, he could instigate a discussion about it—not point any fingers, of course, but just try to get a general sense from them how they used social media and what they thought their responsibilities were.

Yet, even while he considered these options, resentment flared toward the woman who was a thorn in his side at every turn, it seemed.

Claire's phone rang. She answered and murmured a few words, then clicked her phone off and put it back in her purse. She looked slightly anxious.

"This has been fun," she said to the girls, "but I'm sorry. I really have to go."

Sam was slightly taken aback by the wave of concern that rushed through him.

You want her to leave, remember?

But he followed after her.

"Is it your little girl?" he asked. "Is everything okay?"

She stopped and looked at him with a slightly wary expression on her face, like she expected judgment from him for being a single mother. Despite everything, he did admire her for being strong enough to do it on her own and wished that he could tell her that, but they didn't have that kind of connection.

Then she lifted her chin and squared her shoulders, looking him directly in the eyes.

"If you're so concerned," Claire retorted, her eyes spitting fire and her color flaring to red, "then stop getting in the way of me trying to provide a good life for her."

She turned without another word and left.

Standing there, pondering Claire's parting words and fearing there was some truth in them, Sam felt far too alone.

Chapter Two

Driving home, Claire regretted her parting words to Sam and knew she had to work on her trait of speaking first and thinking later. She knew it had to do with her trust issues and had learned how fear could manifest itself by anger. She had prayed often to the Lord about it but still fell back into old habits when she was rattled.

It had been a strange encounter at the church all the way around, which set her off balance. Oh, who was she kidding? Sam Meyer set her off balance most of the time. It would be easier if she could just flat-out dislike him because they couldn't agree on anything if their lives depended on it. But sometimes she couldn't help admiring his intelligence and his commitment to what he believed in, at least when it came to his preaching and how kindly he treated the youth. Also, he wasn't half bad to look at... not that she wanted to look.

All she knew was that her worst self made an appearance whenever she was around him.

But now it was time to get home to Maggie, who, as Rachel had reported, was starting to ask for her mom and showing signs of a meltdown.

There was nothing and no one in the world that captured Claire's heart the way her wiry daughter did, with her eyes that mingled hazel in with Claire's shade of aqua, her dark brown curls and her surprisingly sophisticated vocabulary.

When naming Maggie—her full name was Margaret Rose—Claire had thought about things that brought her joy and immediately she thought of the books she had loved, from *Goodnight Moon* to *Gone with the Wind*, and, of course, her flower shop.

Whenever she was getting close to home, Claire experienced both a surge of joyful anticipation at the thought of seeing Maggie and a tug of regret that she wasn't returning to a house with a big yard that her little girl could play in.

She needed to expand Love Blooms—there was no question about it. She didn't care about having a lot of money for the sake of having it, but she knew what it would take to be able to provide that kind of home for Maggie one day. Not to mention, she wanted to make sure her daughter got a good education, along with food and clothing, and be able to pay for the hobbies and interests she would develop as she got older—and there was no denying that being able to make more money was a sheer necessity.

Just before she opened the door, Claire paused and sent up a spontaneous prayer that she would be able to provide Maggie with the future she deserved. Then, with her heart eager in anticipation of seeing her little girl, she went in.

"I'm home," she called out.

"In the kitchen," Rachel answered, and then Maggie was hurtling toward her, so Claire barely had time to get her arms open before Maggie made impact.

"Oof!" she said, playing it up for her daughter's enjoyment. "Are you a girl or are you a truck?"

"I'm not a truck," Maggie giggled. "But," she added thoughtfully, "I suppose I could imagine I was."

"Yes, you could." Claire hugged her, breathing in her special Maggie scent of oatmeal cookies and baby shampoo.

"I missed you," Maggie said, like she did every day. She said it matter-of-factly, but still, it always caused a ripple of guilt to run through Claire.

When she expanded her business and could hire more staff, she promised herself for the umpteenth time that she would be able to take more time off to spend with her little girl.

For now, she answered as she always did. "I missed you, too. I heard you were working on your Christmas list. You'll have to fill me in."

"I will," Maggie answered. "I think it's a good mix of practical and fun things."

Claire smiled and wondered how she managed to leave this girl every day. Why would she postpone coming home for any reason? Maybe it hadn't been the best decision to agree to drive Troy, especially with what had happened while she was at the church.

But, no, they lived in a community and Claire wanted to help out when and where she could. She wasn't immune from needing support from others and she wanted to set an example for Maggie about caring for others.

Still, she also never wanted Maggie to doubt that she was her number one priority.

"Come on." Claire took Maggie's hand. "Let's have supper."

"The meltdown passed?" she said quietly to Rachel while Maggie slid into her chair.

Rachel nodded as she began serving salad into bowls, while Claire gave the pasta a final stir.

"Yeah, she's a good kid," Rachel said. "She just had a

moment. You were a little later than I expected, but that's okay," she added hurriedly.

"I appreciate you so much, Rachel," Claire said, as her insides did a little twist. She knew it wasn't fair to expect her sister to be a full-time caregiver, especially when she was also encouraging Rachel to find work that utilized her creative skills.

"I want to eat," Maggie grumbled.

"We will, Magpie," Claire said, "Let's give thanks first."

They held hands and said a grace that Maggie had known practically from the time she'd been talking. Then Claire served them all some pasta and salad, and they ate in silence for a minute or two, calming their hunger pangs.

"So you were dropping Troy off," Rachel began as she speared a piece of cucumber with her fork, "and then what happened?"

Claire glanced at Maggie, who was frowning at a rebellious noodle that refused to stay on her fork. Then she summarized the events at the church as she had seen them and her suspicion that there could be some online bullying going on.

"Bullying is mean," Maggie said, reminding Claire that her daughter was always paying attention, even when it didn't look that way.

"You're absolutely right." She tickled her fingers across Maggie's cheek.

Satisfied at being acknowledged, Maggie returned her attention to her food.

"What did Pastor Sam have to say?" Rachel asked, with a glint in her eye that made Claire uneasy because Rachel was prone to reading something into their tension that simply wasn't there.

"Not too much," she said. "He made it pretty clear, though,

that he didn't want my input." Annoyance at the pastor threatened to bubble up and spoil her time with family.

"Really? I can't picture him being rude."

"Oh, he's never rude." Claire wrinkled her nose as she thought of his soft-spoken, well-articulated arguments that poked holes in everything she wanted to accomplish. "He's far too polite for that."

How could she explain that his politeness stirred up a strong urge in her to pick a fight with him? It didn't even make sense to her.

All she knew was that he was constantly putting up barriers in the way of her goals by putting forth his own ideas for the property by Love Blooms, and she didn't care for it, not one bit.

She especially didn't care that she knew his ideas to help the refugee communities were selfless and meaningful. She wanted to do whatever she could for them, too, but not at the expense of achieving what she wanted for her and Maggie's future, or expressing the creative gifts God had given her.

After Claire had helped Maggie with her bath and into her pj's, and listened carefully to her Christmas wish list, she returned to the kitchen and began cleaning up.

She always loved the peaceful feeling of being home safe with her loved ones while the cold darkness lingered outside, holding the promises of the season.

"I still think Sam seems like a decent guy," Rachel said, picking up a towel to dry dishes and continuing the unwanted conversation.

"I'm not saying he's not," Claire sighed. "But it's not like we're going to suddenly become best friends. We can't agree on anything."

"Mom always says that opposites attract," Rachel said teasingly.

But Claire couldn't even handle joking about it. She was too afraid of what the future held for her and Maggie if she couldn't achieve her goal, and there was no way there would ever be any attraction between her and the man who was stopping her from doing that.

"Can we talk about something else?" she said. "Tell me what art projects you've been working on."

Rachel began to describe some abstract butterfly patterns she was working on that she thought might be perfect for greeting cards.

Claire listened and nodded, murmuring encouragement, grateful that the focus had turned away from her and especially away from Pastor Sam.

When the kitchen was clean, Rachel went to her room and Claire attempted to release the tensions of the day by settling in the living room with a book of poetry she was reading. She liked to pick it up, open it to a random page and savor whatever waited for her there. Claire loved the home she shared with Rachel and Maggie. The decor was a combination of the bright colors that she liked and Rachel's creative flair in the artistic touches.

Maggie's room paid an eclectic but heartfelt tribute to her own and some of Claire's childhood favorites, from *Winnie-the-Pooh* to the Narnia books.

Claire read one poem and had just turned the page to begin reading another one when Rachel's bedroom door opened again.

Claire glanced away from her book. She could use the quiet time to sort out her thoughts and regroup for whatever challenges tomorrow held, but she knew that Rachel sometimes needed to talk about her own future and she would never say no to her sister, who helped out so willingly with Maggie.

But it turned out that Rachel still had Sam on her mind, because she said, "Did I ever tell you that I went to Pastor Sam for counseling a few months ago?"

The hand that was still holding the book of poetry involuntarily jerked a little and Claire closed the book and set it carefully on the table beside her.

"What about?" she asked.

"About being worried that I'm never going to find something that I love doing and that I can make a living at," Rachel said. "I know we've talked about that and you're really encouraging and all, but I thought it couldn't hurt to get an outside perspective."

"I didn't know that he was someone you trusted that way." Claire mentally batted away a sense of betrayal. "Was he…? Did it help at all?"

Rachel shrugged. "Somewhat, I guess. I mean, things are still the same with me. He was probably one of the best listeners I've come across. It's just hard…"

"Well…I'm glad you felt like you could talk to him," Claire said, hoping she sounded like she meant it.

"I think you'd also find him good to talk to," Rachel said, not quite making eye contact.

"We talk plenty," Claire reminded her.

"You talk *at* each other and over each other," Rachel said placidly. She plunked herself down on the end of the couch closest to the chair that Claire was curled up in. She helped herself to one of the candy canes that stood up in a vase on the table.

Claire made a mental note that they should put up their tree soon. Maggie loved doing that, but not as much as she loved setting out the Nativity scene, rearranging the figures several times in the days leading up to Christmas.

"I think if you talked *to* each other," Rachel said, "you might actually like each other."

"That's not going to happen," Claire said, not liking the warmth that crept into her cheeks. "We can't agree on anything."

"But wouldn't it get boring if you were with someone who just agreed with everything you said and didn't challenge you?" Rachel asked.

With being a single mother and trying to not only run, but also expand a business, Claire's plate was too full for a relationship anyway. Still, Rachel's observation struck a chord with her.

"Maybe you're right," she conceded.

"Of course I'm right," Rachel said calmly.

"Tell me more about your day," Claire said, pointedly redirecting the conversation. "What's on your wish list for Christmas?"

While Rachel discussed her Christmas wish list, Claire couldn't get her sister's observations about Sam out of her head, and that was the last thing she needed. She wouldn't say she was plagued by anxiety, but juggling the important commitments in her life could undeniably cause stress.

That was one of the reasons she loved flowers and her flower shop so much: she could arrange a bouquet, see the colors, some soft, some vibrant, breathe in the different scents, focus on the movement of her hands, until she was soothed by the rhythm of it all. It also helped to renew her love and awe of God, who created so much beauty for the world to enjoy.

Surely, God would be with her in her longing to expand Love Blooms. Numerous times a day she reminded herself that God understood that she needed to provide for Maggie, and maybe give Rachel some employment, too. She wasn't doing any of it for selfish reasons, but sometimes, whether intentionally or not, Sam's arguments made her second-guess that.

But, no, she mentally argued back. Pastor Sam wasn't the only one who wanted to help others. It was just that her giving had to start closer to home.

Rachel eventually returned to her room and Claire did her best to focus on her reading again. But try as she might, she couldn't stop her thoughts from drifting back to Rachel's comments about her and Sam actually having a conversation. She tried to tell herself that her sister had too vivid an imagination. But Rachel wasn't prone to making needlessly speculative comments about the relationships and emotions of others.

Restlessness churned within Claire, as her attention bounced between checking online for any flower orders that had come in and wondering if she should phone Shirley to see how Troy's evening had turned out. But it had been such a disconcerting experience all around that she didn't want to raise it with Troy's mother. Maybe Troy really had just been in a mood.

A chime signaled a text coming in and Claire had the unbidden thought that maybe it was Sam reaching out to her about what had transpired earlier.

But why would she want him to?

The number wasn't one she recognized, but the message that accompanied it said: Hello, Claire. This is Dorothy Larsen. I hope you don't mind that I got your number from Shirley Allen. We curl together. I was hoping you would call me to discuss the possibility of you doing the flowers for our daughter Patrice's winter wedding.

Claire clutched the phone to her lightly pounding heart. This could potentially be a big order, one that could make a real difference to Love Blooms' bottom line, but she had to stay calm and be professional. But it was difficult to stop the singsong of anticipation that was surging through her, because if things went well, this would be one big step toward her ultimate goal.

Thank You, God, thank You. But please help me not to jump ahead in my thoughts and please guide my words when I talk to Dorothy.

The Larsens were known to be Living Skies' wealthiest family. Tony Larsen was a successful investment banker in Regina, but preferred the small-town life, so he chose to commute instead of living in the city.

Claire didn't know Dorothy Larsen well, but they had served on church council together and were sometimes in the church kitchen together after Sunday services, taking their turns at serving cookies and coffee during the fellowship hour. She perceived Dorothy to be a quiet-spoken but precise woman, who had clear ideas about what she wanted.

Their daughter's engagement to a rising star in the restaurant business had caused quite a stir, and the wedding was anticipated to be a gala event with no expenses spared.

And now Claire had been presented with the opportunity to do flowers for the wedding, something that, if it worked out, would surely bring her dream of expanding her business closer to reality.

She took a deep breath and, praying, decided to phone Dorothy instead of texting back.

"Oh, Claire," Dorothy answered in a low, well-articulated voice. "Thank you so much for getting back to me so quickly."

"I was happy to get your message," Claire said.

They had a brief conversation that touched on Patrice's wedding colors and her favorite flowers. Then Dorothy said, "Of course, we'll want to meet in person as soon as possible and then you'll want to touch base with Pastor Meyer."

"Pastor Meyer," Claire repeated. "Sam Meyer?"

"Yes. You know him, don't you?" Dorothy asked, then answered her own question, chuckling at herself. "Of course you do—from church."

Claire didn't add that she knew him from town-council meetings as well, where they were constantly butting heads.

She took a breath, then asked, "I don't mean to question how you are doing things, but why do I need to talk to the pastor about my flower arrangements?"

Dorothy laughed softly again. "I thought you might ask that, but Sam is much more than a pastor to us. He's also a trusted family friend and adviser."

Claire was silent, listening but still not quite understanding what it was that Dorothy was asking of her. But she didn't want to lose this opportunity, so she literally tightened her lips so that her questions didn't spill out in a manner that might cause her to do just that.

"The flower arrangements will be all up to you, of course," Dorothy said, which was somewhat reassuring. "That is, if when you meet with Patrice and me, we all decide that we can work together. But I don't think it ever hurts to get outside input, do you? It was actually Patrice's wish that Pastor Sam be involved—at least to offer his opinion—on all aspects of the wedding. She trusts him without question and so do I."

Claire tried to remind herself again of what doing the flowers for the wedding of the year could mean to her and Maggie's—and perhaps Rachel's—future, but at the moment all she could imagine was her making flower arrangement after flower arrangement and Pastor Sam Meyer finding fault with every single one.

Sam was sure God must have better things for him to do than meet Dorothy and Patrice Larsen at Murphy's Restaurant to talk about flower arrangements, especially after the almost sleepless night he'd had. Some nights he could stop the misgivings that tormented him but more often not.

But the Larsens were a good family, who had willingly opened their hearts and home to him. He should be honored that they respected his opinion so much, even if it was on matters that were far beyond his areas of expertise.

It was Saturday afternoon, and still the events of the Wednesday-night youth group troubled him. Claire Casey had managed to put doubts into his head that now refused to go away. No matter how much he tried to tell himself that he knew the kids in town, and in the youth group, and that they weren't malicious, the truth was that no one could really know the heart of another person. And he was the prime example of that, keeping his depression under wraps while he encouraged the congregation to find their joy in the Lord.

Sometimes he wondered how it would feel to actually tell someone the absolute truth about his depression and how it impacted him. Would it be like a cold glass of water quenching his thirst, or would he feel even more dried up? Whatever the answer was, at this point, he wasn't willing to risk it.

But the Larsens were counting on him and he wouldn't let them down, even if he wasn't sure how he could help. He experienced a pang each time he remembered that he planned on leaving Living Skies if he was called to a bigger city, but it never seemed like the right time to mention it or that there was any point to doing so when the call hadn't come yet.

Sam arrived at Murphy's Restaurant, a popular eating spot with a cozy atmosphere and homestyle recipes, in good time, and as he opened the door, the smells of coffee and cinnamon buns wafted out to greet him. He could imagine they were tantalizing, but the nocturnal emotional battle he'd wrought left him with little appetite.

The beverages also carried the seasonal notes of Christmas, with the scents of cinnamon and peppermint permeating the air.

"Good morning, Pastor," Michelle, a quiet Indigenous young woman, and one of his favorite servers, said. He admired her for continuing to hold down a part-time job while taking classes online that she needed to become a speech pathologist.

"Good morning, Michelle. I'm meeting Dorothy and Patrice Larsen."

"Oh, they're sitting over there," Michelle said and pointed.

Sam thanked her and headed in that direction.

He didn't usually do well in jam-packed venues, but something about Murphy's made him feel at home, although it was a far cry from the elegant tea shops and muted restaurants that his parents had favored. Then again, maybe that was why he liked it.

Sam's gaze landed at a third person at the table and his heart skipped. He would recognize those determined shoulders, that long neck and the shining dark hair anywhere. It wasn't surprising that Claire would be here on a Saturday morning—almost everyone was—but why was she sitting with the Larsens?

Whatever she was saying was causing Dorothy's rather austere face to be wreathed in a smile, while Patrice, an attractive young woman with long, smooth, carefully highlighted blond hair, leaned in eagerly and was listening to whatever Claire was saying.

The logical part of Sam knew it made sense. They were there to discuss flowers, so naturally a florist would be there. In fact, it made a lot more sense for Claire to be there than for him. For an instant, he considered quietly backing out and making his excuses later. But he knew that wouldn't be the right thing to do.

Besides, now Dorothy had spotted him and, still smiling, waved him over.

"Pastor Sam, I'm so glad you're here." Patrice stood up and gave him a quick hug.

"You can't get married," Sam told her in a teasing voice. "If you're old enough to get married, that means that I'm *really* old."

Sometimes he marveled himself at the persona he was able to present. No one who saw him joking with Patrice would guess what will and how many prayers it had taken to even get him out the door.

Patrice giggled and gestured him to sit beside her. When he did, he was directly across from Claire, and by her slightly skeptical but not startled expression, he guessed that his presence wasn't a surprise to her.

She's not thrilled to see me...

He expected as much, which didn't explain why that notion still stung a little.

Sam darted a glance around the table. The thought had sounded so loudly in his own mind, he was momentarily panicked that he might have said it out loud. But the three women were chatting again, as Claire pointed out some things in a brochure that was open on the table.

He had to say something, though—if nothing else, to figure out exactly what Patrice wanted his role to be, other than performing the ceremony.

Sam cleared his throat and reached for his water glass.

"How's Maggie?" he asked to fill the silence. "What's she up to this morning?"

Claire looked slightly startled, then recovered. "She's good," she said. "When I left, she was helping her aunt make pancakes." She paused, then added, "Thank you for asking."

Michelle came to their table, ready to take his order.

The others weren't eating and Sam was glad of an excuse to just order black coffee.

"Don't get me wrong, Patrice... Dorothy." He looked from one to the other to include them. "You know I love you like family and I'm honored that you value my opinion, but when it comes to your flowers, you've got an expert right here."

"Finally something you and I can agree on," Claire said and then immediately flushed over her impulsive words. "I'm not bragging about my abilities," she explained quickly. "It's just that flower arrangements are my job, and...well, Pastor Sam has his job."

Sam had to admit that he couldn't have said it better himself.

"As I've said," Dorothy began, in a low but persistent voice that reminded Sam of his mother, "we are not suggesting in any way that you do the flower arrangements, Sam. Patrice values you, and so do her father and I. We trust that you will make this wedding, every aspect of it, a day that brings joy to the couple and glory to the Lord, who brought them together."

"Are you asking me to...supervise?" With some effort, Sam managed not to make his voice squeak at the end of the question. It would be almost laughable if it wasn't so unsettling to think about pointing out flaws in the work of a woman who already could barely stand him. Not that he was inclined to do that; he found Claire's flower arrangements to be stunning, creative and thoughtful. There were even moments, when she wasn't glaring at him across the table at Town Hall, hands balled on her hips, that he could see how the arrangements reflected their maker.

He was trying to think of a way that he could excuse himself from all involvement other than premarriage counseling and performing the wedding ceremony, but how could he do that without offending them?

"That sounds fine to me."

Sam thought he must have imagined it, because it didn't sound at all like the kind of thing Claire would say.

He looked across the table at her and her face was impassive. But then he saw the merest glimmer in her eyes that told him that she enjoyed catching him off guard. The question was, why?

"I'm so glad to hear you say that," Dorothy said. "I knew you would understand, Claire. I'll leave it to the two of you to decide how you're going to coordinate things. Is anyone besides me craving something sweet? I'd love to share one of their famous giant shortbreads, if there are any takers."

Patrice nodded. Then her phone chimed and she picked it up. "It's Eric," she said, smiling fondly at her device as she tapped in a reply.

"Ah, young love," Dorothy said. "Maybe being involved in wedding planning will give you some thoughts on settling down, Pastor Sam." She gave him a coy look.

Without meaning to, he looked across the table at Claire and then immediately regretted it as Dorothy's glance followed his own.

Claire's eyes widened and she frowned slightly.

"Oh, that's right," Dorothy said delightedly. "You're single, too, aren't you, Claire? Wouldn't it be wonderful to have a father figure for that precious little girl of yours? Well, we never know what the Good Lord has planned for us, do we?"

"No, we don't," Claire said. Although her voice was steady, her eyes told a different story. She looked annoyed, as he had expected she would, but there was something else there, too—something deep, and sad and regretful.

He realized that he didn't know Claire, not in any kind of real way. She was the undeniably attractive, take-charge woman who tantalized his every last nerve at virtually every encounter he'd ever had with her. But he didn't know her heart, or her dreams—beyond the one of expanding her flower shop, which would involve using the property that he wanted to put to use for those who would truly benefit from it. Also, according to what Rachel had told him, she was an excellent mother and a caring and selfless older sister.

But he had no idea whether she'd ever been married, or wanted to be, and it wasn't his place to know—or to care—other than, of course, with the kind of interest he'd have for any member of the congregation.

"You've gone awfully quiet, Sam," Patrice said. "Mom, you shouldn't tease people like that."

"Who said I was teasing?" Dorothy said, but with a smile. She looked at her watch. "Oh, dear, it's later than I thought. I'm afraid I'm going to have to pass on the shortbread. Patrice and I have a meeting about the invitations. I'm still hoping to convince her to go with something a little less trendy. You can never go wrong with the classic approach, is what I always say."

Patrice rolled her eyes, making her look too young to be a bride.

"I have to get going, too." Claire hastily stood up and gathered her brochures, jamming them into her purse. Clearly, Sam thought, she had no desire whatsoever to be left alone with him.

Which made him ask the question again— why, exactly, had she agreed so readily to work with him when every look and gesture told a different story?

Chapter Three

Why in the world had she agreed to work with Pastor Sam Meyer? He had presented an opportunity to bow out, and, together, they might have been able to convince Dorothy that it wasn't necessary for them to team up on the flowers, while not losing the chance to do the flowers for the wedding.

Was she motivated only by the lucrative opportunity, or was there something else to it, like the fact that she enjoyed throwing him off his game?

Claire studied her face in the mirror, as she smoothed her hair back into a tidy ponytail, as if she hoped her reflection knew more than she did.

Of course it's the only reason, she answered herself. *What other reason could there possibly be?*

But the expression on the face in the mirror said that she wasn't sure.

Do you know why I'm always doing laundry? Claire remembered her mother asking the question on occasion when she and Rachel were growing up. *Because it's my least favorite chore*, she would promptly answer herself. In other words, don't put off the unpleasant tasks, because they will always be there waiting.

Which was why, by the time she got home from Murphy's, she had already decided to call Sam and set up a meeting with him. It would mean leaving Love Blooms closed a little while longer, which wasn't great on a Saturday. But there really wasn't a day that would work better to get this kind of thing done and she was hopeful that a few steps back would result in some big steps forward.

If he was surprised to hear from her so soon after they'd left the restaurant, he hid it well. They agreed to meet at his office. Murphy's Restaurant was a great place to meet and visit, but it wasn't conducive to the kind of discussion they needed to have.

More importantly, after what Dorothy had teased about, she didn't want to give anyone the wrong impression by the two of them showing up there again, and she was sure that Sam would feel the same way.

Well, at least we can agree on that much.

Rachel and Maggie were watching a fishing show on television.

"Fishing?" she teased.

"It's relaxing," Rachel said. "You'd be surprised how creative ideas can pop into my mind when I'm focused on something else."

Claire took a deep breath but then refrained from asking how the job search was going. As always, she felt caught between needing and appreciating Rachel being there for Maggie and knowing that her sister had to find work.

"I think the fish are kind of yucky," Maggie said in a confiding tone. "But Aunt Rachel said in a little while we can go for a walk and look at lights."

"Thank you for this," Claire said. Although she knew Rachel would already be caring for Maggie because Claire opened her shop on Saturdays, she didn't want her sister to ever think that she took her availability for granted.

"It's no problem," Rachel said. She looked away from

the fishing show with a spark of interest on her face. "But I don't really get why you have to meet with Pastor Sam. You're just doing the flowers, aren't you?"

"I am," Claire said, "if they decide they want me to after I show them some of my work. It's hard to explain—I don't totally get it myself—but it sounds like Sam has been a friend and a spiritual mentor to their family for a long time and Patrice wants his input on all aspects of the wedding."

"Your flowers are *bee-you-tiful*, Mommy," Maggie said, reminding Claire once again that she could never assume that her daughter wasn't paying attention.

She would always need to be careful that she didn't express her mixed emotions about the pastor, because she wanted Maggie to have a positive view of the church and respect for the people who shepherded them.

"But not as beautiful as you," Claire said, drawing Maggie into a hug and nuzzling her neck.

Maggie giggled and squirmed. "I have to use the bathroom."

"Then you'd better go use it," Claire said. "I'll be gone by the time you're done, so quick kiss and I'll see you later."

Maggie planted a kiss on Claire's cheek and scampered from the room.

"Sam's okay with chiming in on the flowers?" Rachel asked with a small smile.

"I don't think he's any more thrilled about it than I am," Claire said. "But he doesn't want to offend their friendship. Anyway, I'd better get going. Give Maggie another hug and kiss from me and I'll see you both later."

Claire prayed as she drove to the church. She prayed that the discussion with Sam would go well and, mostly, that it would go quickly. She pulled into a parking spot—even

on a Saturday there were a few cars in the parking lot—
then turned off the engine and breathed slowly in and out.

It was only a meeting. It could be over in ten minutes,
probably less. What was she so nervous about?

She could only answer herself that being around Sam
Meyer always set her on edge. It would be easier if she
could flat-out convince herself that he had no redeeming
qualities, but if he wasn't so inclined to argue against almost everything that came out of her mouth, she might be
able to admit that he had qualities she admired.

But she would never admit the way the sudden smile that
completely altered his solemn face made her heart somer-
sault in response.

As Claire walked down the hallway, she thought again
about the strange happenings at the youth group from the
previous Wednesday night. She hoped that whatever had
upset Jason had been taken care of, and that Troy's sullen
silence just stemmed from a bad day. She didn't have any of
her own experience parenting a teen—at least not yet—but
from listening to parents at church, at the gym and in her
shop, she gathered that teens tended to be moody.

But she couldn't quite convince herself. She may not
be the parent to a teen yet, but she had *been* a teen herself,
and unfortunately, she did know from experience that they
could be unkind to each other.

It still wasn't easy being an overweight woman in a society that generally embraced slimness as a standard of
beauty, but at least now she had the confidence to embrace
her own style and to make healthy choices about food and
exercise, not to fit into a mold but because it was what made
her feel best. But as a teen, she hadn't yet gained that kind
of confidence and some memories were still painful.

She wondered if that was another reason why the pastor's challenges against her goals felt so personal.

When Claire got to Sam's office, he was sitting at his desk and she paused in the doorway before announcing herself.

He was absently roughing up his hair with one hand while he studied whatever he had up on his computer screen, and the resulting disarray gave him a boyish look that made a jumble of her insides, which was puzzling in juxtaposition to their rivalry.

She tapped lightly on the frame of the open door. "I'm here," she said. He looked up, and if she hadn't known better, his smile would have made her believe that he was glad to see her.

It's just his after-church smile, she reminded herself, even while her heart responded to that smile with its usual gymnastics.

"Please sit down." Sam gestured to a chair, interrupting her scrambled thoughts, which was probably a good thing. "I don't think this has to be a long meeting."

Immediately, Claire's shoulders tightened, even though she had just been thinking the same thing. Except when Sam said it, it was like he had already decided the way things were going to be.

"Are you going to sit?" It wasn't until he asked the question that she realized she was still standing, clutching her purse tightly in both hands. She sat down, but perched on the edge of the chair, her back erect.

"Is that—" he gestured to her purse "—a reindeer?"

She quickly folded her arms around it. "It makes me smile."

"I like it," Sam said. "It suits you."

Claire thought she could hardly have been more surprised if he'd gotten down on one knee and asked her to marry him. She wouldn't have imagined that the argumentative pastor put any thought into what suited her and what didn't.

But is he implying that he thinks I'm silly?

Before she could ponder that further, his next words surprised her even more.

"Basically, I agreed to this meeting so that I can tell Dorothy and Patrice that we met and talked about things. I want you to know that I have no intention of putting my nose where it doesn't belong. Flowers are your thing and you always do a remarkable job, so whatever you do, I'll tell them it has my blessing."

In the midst of sorting out this unexpected declaration— *he thinks I do a remarkable job?*—the unintentional phrasing registered with Claire and she giggled.

"Something is funny?" Sam asked, with a puzzled expression.

"You said you had no intention of putting your nose in— and I was just thinking of flowers and how people like to smell them." She snorted and blushed.

But then Sam laughed, too, and Claire realized it was a rare sound. He did have a nice laugh, warm and sincere. The briefly shared laughter somehow made the resumed silence between them even more awkward.

"Is there really a blessing for flowers?" Claire asked to fill that silence.

"The scriptures have plenty to say about God the creator and the beautiful world He creates for us," Sam said. "That applies to flowers, too."

"Actually, that's one of my favorite scriptures," Claire said musingly. "The one in Romans that talks about how God is so apparent in nature that we really have no excuse not to believe He exists. I often think of it when I'm working with my flowers."

"Romans One, Verse Twenty," Sam said, then quoted it. Claire nodded.

"I think about that when I'm questioning if I made the right decision to open a flower shop," she said. "It's not easy running a business and I admit it won't be easy to expand," she added deliberately. "But then I can reassure myself that I'm doing my best to reflect God's image when I work."

"And I can reassure myself of the same thing," Sam said, his own pointed tone making it clear that whatever bonding may have happened between them over their shared laughter and her favorite scripture was destined to be short-lived.

"I know I'm doing the right thing by welcoming the strangers among us."

Claire clenched her purse in both hands. "You think you're better than me," she accused.

Sam shook his head, frowning. "It has nothing to do with that, and for the record, no, I don't." He sighed and shook his head, closing his eyes briefly.

Claire imagined he was wishing she would just disappear.

He opened them again. "Look, I just wanted to tell you that I'm not going to interfere with your doing flowers for Patrice's wedding, if the Larsens decide that's what they want. I'm not sure how we got so off track."

He stood up behind his desk, a pale imitation of his after-service smile on his lips, and extended his hand.

"So, can we wrap things up?"

But Claire didn't take his hand. Much as she was more than ready to go herself, and didn't want to delay opening Love Blooms any longer than she had to, she found herself once again pushing back against what Sam wanted.

It didn't help that his dismissal stung even more after she'd allowed herself to enjoy his warm laughter and hearing him quote a scripture that was so meaningful to her in his warm, vibrant voice.

But their dispute over what was best for the property had reared its head again almost immediately.

That was nothing new, so why was it causing such an acute wave of disappointment?

She held her purse in front of her like it was a shield and asked, "Why don't you like me?"

Sam physically jerked in surprise. He knew that Claire Casey was forthright, but he didn't expect this. Despite their constant clashing of wills, it never occurred to him that she would take it personally. And for that, he was currently bemoaning his lack of insight. Granted, he didn't have a lot of experience dealing with the emotions of women, except for in his professional role as a counselor. He was an only child, so hadn't grown up with any sisters, and his mother was a paragon of modulated behavior, even behind the doors of their home. So nothing prepared him for a woman like Claire, who put it all out there.

On some level he was sure he should—and could—admire that. But right now it was taking all of his self-control not to blurt out that he'd had a horrible night and he really, *really* could not deal with this additional pressure.

But he was a pastor and, personal rivalry aside, Claire was a member of the congregation and, more to the point, a human being. He couldn't exactly make a case for being welcoming to strangers if all he wanted to do was push her away.

Lord, I do not like what this woman does to me.

Whatever his thoughts and inner struggles were, though, it was clear she wasn't going anywhere until she got an answer.

"I don't dislike you," he said, hating how stiff and distant he sounded—often a product of tamping down turbulent emotions—and how inadequate the words were. "If you're referring to our...disagreements at the town-council meetings, that's just business. I didn't know you felt personally attacked and I'm genuinely sorry for that."

He almost wished he could say more, tell her about his depression, talk to her about his plans to leave Living Skies.

That would probably make her day.

But those weren't doors he was willing to open yet. Besides, if he told her he didn't even plan to stay in Living Skies, she would question his insistence on using the property for something other than her flower-shop expansion and maybe she'd be right to do so. He only knew that it was important to him to try to make a difference wherever he was. No, he reminded himself, it was more than important. It was imperative, if he wanted to not only make a difference but prove himself worthy of a larger congregation.

Claire was silent for a moment, but then instead of getting up, she settled comfortably in the chair, signaling that she had no intention of leaving until they talked things out.

Please, Lord, I really need Your strength right now.

"Okay, maybe you don't dislike me," Claire said. "But you certainly don't think that what I do is important or meaningful. Like earlier, when I tried to say how I believe my work has value in God's eyes, you immediately had to one-up me with what you're trying to do."

Well, maybe it's the way you said it. But, no, it wouldn't do any good to take the conversation down that path.

"I just told you how much I admire what you do with your flowers," Sam said. "Really, I can't imagine how anyone could do a better job."

"But you don't believe that my flower shop has any real importance," Claire stated firmly.

He disliked being put on the spot by her, yet, in some ways, he couldn't help admiring her gumption. She spoke her mind and let the chips fall where they might.

Someone like that would be good for you.

Sam shook his head in protest, wondering where in the world that thought had come from.

"Are you agreeing or disagreeing that you don't think my flower shop is important?" Claire asked, making Sam aware of his unbidden reaction to his own thoughts.

With effort, he corralled his wandering thoughts and made himself focus on the matter at hand.

"I think that your flower shop offers an important service to Living Skies," he said. "Your arrangements have brought happiness to many people on many different occasions. And you're clearly good at what you do, or Dorothy Larsen wouldn't have asked you to do the flowers for Patrice's wedding."

"With your supervision," Claire interjected.

"I already told you," Sam said, speaking carefully, "I have no intention of supervising, or any desire to. As I've said, you clearly know far more about flower arrangements than I ever will."

"That's all great," Claire said. "But you don't think it's important enough that I should get the space to expand. You don't think that what I do can make a *real* difference in people's lives. Not like what you do."

If she only knew.

Not that he would ever tell anyone this, and especially not Claire Casey, but when there were many days when just getting out of bed felt like an accomplishment, he wasn't exactly in a position to brag about what a difference he made.

But maybe that was why he was so determined to push, to do what he could while he was in Living Skies, and why he was even more determined to shepherd at a larger church.

He chose to ignore the persistent voice within that tried to tell him that he couldn't escape his depression in a larger congregation. Okay, he knew that, but he still couldn't help hoping it might decrease its power over him and maybe it would be easier to hide in a bigger city.

He realized that Claire was studying him, waiting for an answer. She never said anything just for the sake of saying it—he knew that well enough from the meetings they'd both attended. Her tenacity knew no bounds, and that was a trait he admired and might admire even more if it wasn't so often set up as a roadblock against him.

"If you think I don't see what you do for your daughter and sister, and for the town, you're wrong," he said. "I wish I had half of your commitment and energy."

Her striking eyes widened and Sam's heart clenched. He was strangely sad that a compliment from him would surprise her so much, yet based on their interactions, he couldn't really blame her.

She absent-mindedly stroked the antlers of the reindeer on her purse and asked, without looking up, "What are you passionate about aside from your faith?"

The assumption that he was passionate about his faith, or about anything, for that matter, stung, although she would have no way of knowing how his depression could make it seem like he was looking at life through a foggy glass, never seeing things as brightly or as sharply focused as the way he longed to.

Still, there had to be an answer. There must be things that he cared about.

"It wasn't supposed to be a trick question," Claire said,

with a slight humorous edge to her voice. "I just meant, what are your hobbies? What do you do in your spare time when you're not preaching or leading youth group?"

A genuine curiosity lit up her face and his breath stumbled in a way he hadn't expected.

"Wait. Let me guess." She settled back in the chair, making herself comfortable, like she intended to stay a good long while. She truly did have a gift for provoking him.

She tilted her head to one side. "In high school, you were a jock."

Sam shook his head slowly back and forth. "You could not be more wrong."

"Oh? Tell me more."

Sam knew what she was doing. Claire Casey was not the type of person who wanted to leave a room feeling dismissed. Because he had tried to cut their conversation short, she would do everything she could to make it last, just to prove a point.

Something about the way she gazed at him made Sam afraid he was suddenly going to spill all of his secrets.

What was it about her that made it easy to fear that on some level she sensed them? He wanted her to go away. He wanted to close the door and be alone with his thoughts.

"I wasn't much into sports or extracurricular activities," he answered instead, hoping that doing so would expedite the conclusion of the conversation. "I would rather have spent my time reading a book."

It was true, and as far as he was willing to go. There was no way he was going to get into the way depression had impacted his time at school. It took so much effort to keep his head above water that he focused solely on passing his classes. He hadn't had the time or the desire to pursue much else.

Claire looked like she'd been picking at a lock and was a little taken aback to see it finally spring open.

"See, not much of a story." Sam mentally edged the door back shut again, although not completely. "I mean, it wasn't easy being the PK—pastor's kid—but it wasn't the worst place in the world.

"What about you?" he couldn't resist asking, though questioned himself at the same time for prolonging the conversation. Claire had him topsy-turvy yet again. "How did you enjoy school? I guess it's probably different when you go to high school in a small town, where you've known everyone your whole life."

"Well, Living Skies isn't Mayberry," Claire said, referring to a small town from a classic television series, where a big issue could be how quickly a pie would cool before you could eat it.

"I understand people have real problems here."

She leveled her gaze at him. "Yes, I guess you would. I suppose you think that faith solves most of them, though?"

"No," Sam said quietly. "I don't." He had no intention of going down *that* conversational road. Although he was somewhat tempted to see the look on her face if he spilled just how difficult holding on to faith really was for him. He supposed he could go into a ready-made spiel about how God didn't remove all trials, but was with us in our trials, but with Claire, he somehow didn't want to. Instead, he persisted, "I asked about your high school."

"Oh, I was about as popular as any overweight girl," she said.

Her bluntness took him aback, as did her assessment of herself. The words had been spoken carelessly, but he could sense the pain behind them. Maybe that was because his counseling made him proficient at looking past what people showed on the surface, or at least made him aware that there usually was more than what they did show.

He could tell by the way she'd said it that she wasn't looking to be reassured, and she certainly wasn't looking for, nor would she fall for, any false flattery.

So he would tell her the truth as he saw it.

"You are an attractive woman in all ways," he said. "There isn't anything I would change about you."

There, that oughta show her!

Except, instead of feeling like he had proved a point, it felt like he had discombobulated himself, with his emotions flying every which way.

Claire's face softened, making it even more beautiful, but then, as if fearful of letting herself get drawn in, her expression suddenly went harder than he'd ever seen it.

"I don't think the kids at school saw it quite that way," she said, the hand stroking the reindeer's head on her purse the only thing betraying her nerves. "But thank you."

How was it that he, a pastor, a trained counselor and speaker, could say things that always sounded so colossally wrong whenever he was around this woman? He wanted to offer something else—anything—to ease past the clearly upsetting memories he had inadvertently unearthed.

Somehow, now he wanted that more than getting rid of her as quickly as possible.

Dear Lord, I want her to believe that she really is beautiful and for her to see that beauty in herself.

It didn't seem right to just part ways now, even if every natural instinct screamed that was what he wanted to do. For whatever it was worth, they had shared some vulnerabilities, and Sam found he wasn't quite willing to let go of that connection, if only because it might help alleviate some of the tension between them at the next meeting they attended.

"Speaking of tough times at school," he said, not entirely sure where he intended to go with the conversation, "I want you to know that I have been thinking about what you said on Wednesday night—about the possibility that something online upset Jason."

Claire stopped stroking her purse and sat forward, her eyes bright with interest.

"Do you know him? I didn't recognize him from around here."

"Not very well," Sam admitted. "He's from Willow Grove."

Willow Grove was a town about twenty minutes away from Living Skies.

"How did he start coming to your youth group?"

"He just showed up one night. I didn't question it. We get kids in from all over and all are welcome."

"So that wasn't the first time he was there?" Claire mused.

"No," Sam said. "I think it was about his third or fourth time. He's a quiet kid—I mean, not a leader in the group by any stretch, but he always looked like he was enjoying himself and he kept coming back."

Claire nodded thoughtfully. "Did you ask the others anything about him?"

"I tried to," Sam answered. "I skirted around the subject a bit. I didn't want to seem like I was accusing any of them."

Claire straightened her spine. "I don't think you should accuse anyone, but I think it's worth a conversation with the whole group on Wednesday."

Sam wasn't so sure. So they had a difference of opinion on the matter. What else was new? Now he wavered again between thinking they had—or at least could—come to a better understanding of each other and thinking that Claire was sticking her nose in because it was yet another way to challenge him.

"Or maybe Jason will just show up again," he said, "and everything will be fine."

He didn't really believe that. He legitimately couldn't remember a time he honestly believed that everything was fine—quite the opposite. But he was back to wanting this conversation to be over.

"That would be nice for you," Claire said, and in her tone he could hear the pressure of brakes being applied. "I've never known things to just work out for me."

She stood up again. "I think I've kept you long enough."

"Wait, please," Sam said, although he really had no idea why he didn't just let her leave when that was what he had wanted.

"Did you mean what you said?" he asked.

"About what?" Her eyes narrowed.

"About your favorite Bible verse. Does the creation around you really help boost your faith in God?"

She nodded without hesitation, though her eyes clearly questioned why he asked. "Always."

Sam wondered if any of that easy acceptance could possibly rub off on him, and if he was willing to risk more time with the person who ran his thoughts all over the place in order to find out.

"I think I want to be part of what you do for Patrice after all," he said.

"Why?" Claire asked, clearly confused and definitely not pleased.

"I can't fully explain," Sam said. "I've just decided it might be a good idea after all."

Chapter Four

〜

Bright and early on Tuesday morning, Claire impulsively tucked an orange lily into her updo. It was a flower that represented confidence, and if she didn't exactly feel that way, maybe dressing the part might help.

But she doubted it.

She wondered where she was going to start. She was still wondering, in fact, why she had agreed to let Sam come watch her work in the first place, and the only conceivable answer she could give herself was that she wanted the Larsens to know that she was cooperative and willing to work with Sam in whatever way she needed to.

She also wanted Sam to know that he was not going to… Well, she wasn't going to let him do whatever it was he thought he was doing.

She reminded herself that she was doing it all with the hope of giving her and Maggie a decent future.

Christmas was coming, too, and, even though she had smiled at Maggie's list, Claire still wanted to provide her daughter with at least some of the items she wanted.

But now she stood in the middle of her flower shop like she'd never set foot in it before, while Sam, flawlessly punctual, stood in the doorway.

Why he had done a complete turnaround within one

conversation and decided he wanted to be involved in her making the flower arrangements remained a mystery. The only answers that Claire could come up with were that he enjoyed provoking her, or that God was testing her patience in a special kind of way.

Quite possibly both.

"Just do what you always do," Sam said, in a way that made Claire wonder just how long she'd been frozen to the spot. "Pretend I'm not here."

Yeah, like that's so easy to do.

"I, uh, I guess I usually start the day with coffee," Claire said.

"Coffee it is, then." Sam clapped his hands together decisively, reminding her suddenly of him leading youth group, which was a good thing, but also of his well-that's-settled gesture at town-council meetings, which was not so good.

This is my shop, she argued inwardly, as if she'd been asked to defend that fact.

"Can I help?"

The cautious note in Sam's voice chased away at least some of Claire's instinctive defensiveness, as she considered that maybe she wasn't the only one who found this situation awkward.

Still, he was the one who had put them here.

"I make pretty decent coffee, if you want to show me where you keep supplies," Sam added.

"That's okay. I've got it," Claire said hastily. The only thing more unnerving than having Sam in her early morning space to start with would be to rub elbows with him in the kitchen space at the back of the store, which was so small that they could literally do just that.

But his query had at least made her spring into action.

She would make the coffee first, and by the time that was done, she would know what to do next.

Except Sam still stood near the entryway and his body language was becoming more uncertain with each passing second. Suddenly she missed the hand-clapping decisiveness.

"Sit here," Claire said, more bluntly than she'd intended. She beckoned him to a tall stool by a counter where she sat to work on flower arrangements.

Sam did as instructed, and something about him being in her creative space put Claire's stomach in a jumble. It was like she was sharing her secrets without meaning to.

"I'll be right back," she said. She resisted the urge to tell him not to touch anything.

In the small room that passed as a kitchen at the back of the store, Claire watched her hands go through the motions of making coffee. Why couldn't she stop thinking of Sam out in her shop, waiting?

Why couldn't she stop seeing vulnerability in his eyes?

She didn't want to actually care about Sam Meyer's feelings. She had no room for that in her life. She had a daughter to raise and the financial realities that went with that, and she couldn't count on Rachel to meet her childcare needs indefinitely. That wasn't fair to either of them, or to Maggie, who would benefit from more interaction with children her own age.

Claire smiled softly to herself, pausing to think of Maggie, with her eyes magnified by her round glasses, her billowing hair that somehow always smelled of oatmeal-raisin cookies.

She was such a sweet girl and used to being around adults, but Claire didn't want her to miss out on all the things that went with being a kid, either.

But now it was time to face the situation at hand. She didn't want to be so long making the coffee that Sam came looking for her.

When Sam spotted her exiting the back room with a tray, he immediately jumped up and came forward to assist her. Their fingers brushed as he went to retrieve the tray and Claire experienced a disconcerting rush of warmth.

She inadvertently met Sam's eyes and saw a matching confusion there. Then he firmed his grip and she relinquished her hold.

Why did it feel like she had to be careful that wasn't all she was giving up?

After their first few sips of coffee, Claire said, "I guess I should get to work."

Sam nodded encouragingly, but still, the two of them remained, clutching their coffee mugs and looking at one another, uncertain of how to proceed.

"How about you start putting an arrangement together," Sam suggested, "and I can watch and you can explain to me why you've chosen the flowers that you have."

Claire folded her arms and studied him. Was he going to critique her choices? But there was a respectful interest in his eyes.

"Well, for starters," she said, "I don't usually just put an arrangement together. I like to think about the person it's for, their personality and what they might want to express with the arrangement."

"I can tell you some things about Patrice," Sam offered.

With the tension between them, Claire hadn't considered that. "I—I think that might be a good idea," she said.

"Are you actually admitting that I might be helpful?" Sam teased with an undeniably attractive smile.

Claire had a disconcerting sensation of not recognizing

him and realized how seldom she saw him as anything other than serious. He was unfailingly kind with most people; he listened attentively; he smiled politely.

But he's not happy. She was struck by how certain she was of this.

Disconcerted, she turned away and made a show of organizing some small tools she kept nearby for trimming and removing what wasn't needed for the bouquet.

"I was just teasing," Sam said quietly.

Claire turned back to him, telling herself that she really didn't know him at all, although the strange certainty of his unhappiness lingered.

She forced a smile. "I know. So tell me about Patrice."

"May I?" Sam set his coffee on the counter and indicated that he wanted to pull a stool up beside her.

Claire hesitated briefly, though she didn't know why. It wasn't like she was going to refuse to let him sit beside her.

Much as she might want to. His solid presence, combined with his freshly scrubbed scent and vulnerability, made her all too aware of his proximity.

"Okay," she said, trying to sound like she at least believed she was in control. "You talk and I'll work. I have to get some roses dethorned."

"Let's see..." Sam sat on the stool he had pulled over and Claire could smell his pine-scented soap.

"Probably the first thing you need to know about Patrice," Sam continued, "is that she likes things that make her stand out from the crowd."

"Like planning a winter wedding instead of a summer one," Claire said.

Sam nodded.

"She and her mother will be at odds, though," Sam said. "I'm sure you already picked up on that with what Dorothy had to say about the invitations. She'll have equally strong opinions about what makes an appropriate bouquet. I just wanted to give you a heads-up."

Claire wasn't sure what to say. Was he trying to be helpful, or was he discouraging her before she even got started?

No, she dismissed the later thought. Despite whatever else she thought about Sam, he wasn't that kind of person. But she didn't know anyone else who had her constantly guessing which way was up and which way was down, and it was maddening.

"It's Patrice's wedding, though," she said after a moment. "Ultimately, she's the one I want to please."

A slightly troubled expression crossed Sam's face and he looked like he wanted to say more. But then he just said, "Well, if anyone can make it work, I'm sure you can."

He gently nudged her in a wholly unexpected way and Claire promptly jabbed her finger on a thorn of one of the roses.

Well, if she needed any proof that being around Sam Meyer wasn't the best thing for her, it came in the form of a stinging fingertip, where a small droplet of blood now formed.

"Let's have a look." Sam motioned to take her hand, but she pulled it away, then turned her face, ignoring the question in his eyes.

"I wasn't paying attention to what I was doing," she mumbled, embarrassed. "I'm okay."

"You'd better get a bandage," Sam said.

Claire grabbed a tissue from a box nearby and wrapped it around the wound.

"You're bleeding through the tissue. Let me see." Sam held out his hand again and Claire backed away and put her hands behind her back like she was Maggie.

But that wasn't fair to Maggie, who probably would have been much more mature about it.

Sam tilted his head with a bemused expression.

"Please, let me have a look," he said.

I'm being ridiculous.

She brought her hand out and waggled her fingers in front of his face in what she hoped was an airy manner.

It was a pretense that lasted only as long as it took Sam to catch the injured finger in his hand and raise it closer to his face for inspection.

His hand was so warm. She had expected… Well, she didn't know what she had expected, but it wasn't that. They were also more calloused than she would have anticipated, not soft and pampered. She had always disliked pampered-looking hands on men…and on women, for that matter.

"Don't you have any real bandages?" Sam's question brought Claire's thoughts to a halt like so many cars jamming into each other in a pileup.

"I might have some in the back," she said, in a rather haughty tone that tried to mask her embarrassment.

"Hmm," Sam said, in an inspecting kind of way, "it doesn't look too bad. Do you have an antiseptic ointment?"

"I do have some," Claire said in a deliberate manner, "but you're going to have to let me go so that I can get it."

Sam gave his head a brief shake. Then it was almost like he had stepped outside of himself to observe his own actions and saw himself clinging to Claire's hand.

He let go and her breath sucked in, now a reaction to an absence.

But Sam was Sam again, austere and professional.

"I'll, ah, go get this cleaned up and find a bandage," Claire said.

"I'll wait here," Sam said calmly.

As Claire washed her hands, she studied her flushed face in the mirror, asking herself how she was going to work with Sam on the wedding flowers when everything about him set her nerves on edge, even when he was being nice to her—*especially* when he was being nice to her.

She would do it, she answered herself. She would do it because she had to and because his knowledge of the Larsens would help her be successful.

That was what she would think about, not the warmth of his hands and the concern in his eyes.

Sam watched Claire's determined strides from the back of the store and wondered if she had any idea of the glorious picture she made, but suspected that she did not.

He shook away the thought. He wasn't here to admire Claire's beauty, although being aware of it was highly impactful to him because finding pleasure in beauty, or anything else, was always a struggle. He was here to make sure things went smoothly with the Larsens. They trusted his input and were counting on him.

Sure, I'll keep telling myself that.

The truth was, he still wasn't sure exactly what had made him say that he had chosen to stay involved after all, especially after telling Claire he would step aside. But her trust in God because of her flowers was like an invisible hand reaching toward him and offering something he craved but that had always eluded him.

Even though—or maybe because—they hardly seemed able to agree on anything, Sam realized that he did appreciate being around Claire Casey. She challenged him. She made him think about things from a different perspective. Most of all, when he was with her, he was, somehow, pulled outside of his own thoughts, which meant he wasn't perpetually analyzing his levels of happiness or lack thereof.

With Claire he could almost forget his depression, at least for a time.

But there was no way she would ever know this.

"Where's the flower you had in your hair?" he blurted out as she approached him.

She had been walking with purpose, wearing an expression that he thought of as her council-meeting face.

But her expression faltered at his question, which made his heart splinter a little.

Then she lifted her chin in a gesture that was all too familiar to him. "I took it out," she said. "It didn't suit my mood anymore."

"I've heard or read somewhere that different flowers can represent different meanings or emotions," Sam said, after a pause. "Is that true?"

"Yes," Claire said, "that's absolutely true."

He enjoyed watching the passion return to her face as she warmed to her subject, teaching him some of the meanings behind flowers and how she used that knowledge to personalize the flower arrangements she made for her clients.

"I would hope to do the same for Patrice, of course," she said. "You could give me a few words that you best thought described her and I would try to encompass those in the flowers I chose for her bouquet."

"That sounds really nice," Sam said, even as his conscience pricked at him. He loved the Larsens, but he knew how exacting Dorothy could be and he didn't want Claire thinking her doing the arrangements was a sure thing before it was.

"I hear a *but*," Claire said, a stony expression chasing away her previous enthusiasm. "Sam, I'm still really not sure why you changed your mind about being involved in this, when we'd both agreed that it wasn't necessary. But, at the very least, I ask that you trust that I know what I'm doing."

Okay, he could always expect her to be straightforward and, in fact, counted on it, so why did it now feel like a small, stinging slap?

"I love your ideas," Sam replied, trying to sound reassuring. "The only *but* you're hearing is that I don't know yet what kind of decision they are going to make on the flowers."

Why was it that they always butted heads even when he thought they'd been getting along as well as they ever had?

"I guess maybe you've decided to stay involved because the Larsens want your input and you don't want to let them down," Claire said. "But I won't have you in here discouraging me."

"That's not my intent." Sam again hated how he sounded so stiff and formal. "I just don't want you to end up disappointed."

Claire breathed slowly in and out. "If you work with me instead of against me, I don't see any reason why I would have to be."

Sam swallowed a frustrated sigh.

He wanted to tell her that it was never his intention to work against her, even at the town-council meetings, but she would never believe that speaking up for something he believed in didn't have to mean that he was against her or her ideas. And he doubted he could convince her otherwise now.

He wondered if he could possibly tell her that his depression made it hard to believe that anything would work out, or make her understand the other reason his suggested project was so important to him.

No, he answered himself. Things were complicated enough.

"I will do everything I can do to let the Larsens know you're right for this job," he said. "Please believe that."

Claire studied his face for a long moment and he couldn't tell if she trusted him or not.

"Anyway, I'd better get back to work," she said. "It will be time to open the store before we know it."

She resumed her work, taking the time to explain her thoughts and her reasoning behind the flower selections.

There was something about watching Claire demonstrate her creativity that was both energizing and profoundly peaceful.

It reinforced in Sam that dumping about his depression on her wouldn't be the right thing to do. She was raising a beautiful little girl as a single mother and he knew that she also had worries about the future of her sister, Rachel.

There was no way he was going to add to her load, even if he thought for one second she'd be inclined to let him.

What he did blurt out, however, was "I think that watching you work could give me ideas for my sermons."

Claire wrinkled her forehead. "What do you mean?"

"Just that I can see what you mean about sensing God's presence through His creation."

"Well...okay." Something he couldn't quite read glittered behind her cautious expression.

"Honestly, Claire," Sam said, "if it bothers you this much for me to be involved, then I can back away if that's what you really want. But I do know the Larsens and I really do think I can help you."

And I think that you're already helping me.

"How can I convince you?"

She studied him with a tilted head, pursing her lips.

"I guess for starters, you could try being a bit more useful." She handed him a small tool used for removing the thorns from roses.

Sam couldn't help a small grin.

"Did I say something funny?" Claire raised one meticulously shaped dark eyebrow, but he was sure she was fighting back her own smile.

"No, I'm just glad you'll give me a chance."

Soon enough, most of the tension eased out of the room, leaving just enough that Sam put his concentration into what he was doing and didn't try to engage Claire in conversation.

It was sheer pleasure to watch her work, and after a little while the habitual bleakness he experienced seemed to ease a bit.

Her strong, capable hands and long, slender fingers were a marvel in motion, seeming to have almost a mind of their own, as they discarded, rearranged and focused on the finer touches.

"Good job," she said, leaning in close enough to inspect Sam's work so that he could smell the mix of roses and the perfume that was her own clean skin.

It was almost silly how close to happiness the brief compliment brought him. He couldn't remember the last time his heart had experienced such a lift from someone shaking his hand after church and saying, "Good sermon."

Would he really get that kind of reassurance from a bigger church? Somehow, at that moment, he couldn't imagine anything else bringing the relief of a brief light into the constant darkness he battled.

For the first time, he wondered if getting away was really what he needed to be doing.

"Is there anything else I can do?" he asked, not prepared to dwell on that question.

Claire considered the question, gnawing her lower lip. "I don't think so. I probably shouldn't have made you do the roses. You don't actually work here."

"You didn't make me do anything," Sam said. "I was happy to make myself *more useful*." He couldn't help putting some extra emphasis on the final words.

"Yeah, okay…" Claire shrugged. "So you were annoying me."

Sam chuckled and saw the initial surprise and then the shy pleasure on Claire's face.

"You have a nice laugh," she said then. Before he could react, she turned back to what she had been doing.

Was it his imagination, or did he see a faint flush creeping up the back of Claire's lovely neck?

"Thank you," he said quietly to her back.

She didn't reply or turn back to him, but he saw her hands go still over the flowers for just a moment before she resumed her work.

Sam checked the time and saw that he needed to get going soon. He had his own job to do and people needed him to do it well, to be a certain kind of person, one that they could trust and count on.

Not one whose head was filled with thoughts of one particular woman and the world of creative beauty she was part of, and of how that woman and her work made him wonder if there was another way out of his darkness besides trying to disappear into a larger place.

Chapter Five

A few days later, as the time neared for Sam to leave and for Claire to open the shop and get on with the job she was supposed to be doing, she experienced a conflicting mix of emotions that troubled her.

It started when he arrived with a book of poetry with the theme of poems that helped one remember that spring was coming, even in the dead of winter.

"I overheard you saying something once after church about liking poetry," Sam said, handing it to her. Then he added when she was momentarily too bewildered to accept it, "It was on the library sale table and it made me think of you—I mean, of what you do here with your flowers," he quickly amended.

"You heard me say something once about poetry," Claire said, "and you remembered?"

She swallowed with a fleeting but intense urge to cry.

"I hope that's okay," Sam said with an anxious look like he feared he'd crossed a boundary.

"Yes," Claire said, reaching out and accepting the book from him. "Thank you. It's okay. It's very nice of you, thank you."

That morning as they worked, they talked a bit about poetry and other literature, although Sam admitted he wasn't much for poems.

"I like short stories myself," he said.

"I don't mind them," Claire said, "but sometimes they leave me wondering if I've understood what the point is."

"That's pretty much how I feel about poetry all the time," Sam said.

Yet he had seen this book, Claire reflected, and he had bought it knowing that it was something she would enjoy.

She squared her shoulders. She was going to have to watch that she didn't let herself forget they had different and opposing goals.

Still, it had been a kind and unexpected gesture, so as she played with a selection of gerbera daisies, she said, "Sometimes I like to make up stories while I do the arrangements."

"I knew that you like to get to know the people you're doing flowers for," Sam said, looking interested, "but I take it this is something different?"

His attentiveness, while flattering, was rather unnerving, especially when Claire realized she'd opened the door to sharing something within her secret inner world.

"It's kind of silly," she hedged.

"I could use silly," Sam said in all seriousness.

"Okay...well, I like to pretend sometimes that I'm making bouquets for a fairy-tale princess and I have to make the perfect bouquet to save the kingdom..."

She stopped, feeling a flush color her cheeks. "See, I told you—silly."

But Sam's eyes held more affection than she'd ever seen in them.

"Confession time?" he asked.

"Sure." Although she wasn't sure, not at all. She wondered if he was going to try to appease her awkwardness by sharing something about himself.

So, she was surprised when instead he said, "I've been following your website for a little while now."

"Thank you," Claire said, unsure of how she was meant to respond. "I can use all the followers I can get."

"I just want to let you know, I think that all the kingdoms are safe in your hands."

It was like the wall that was between them, or at least several bricks, was starting to tumble and Claire had to struggle hard not to let herself forget how much she needed the space to expand and that her plans in life were to give her daughter a future, not to get thrown off track by some kindness and good conversation.

She had worked hard, cutting corners, using thrift shops when possible for her and Maggie's clothes, looking for marked-down specials at the grocery store, banking every extra penny she could to save money.

Sam was getting bolder, too, in making suggestions and asking questions. Claire had to admit that he had an eye for what worked. But then, he had confessed to finding her shop online.

So he looked for me.

Even a few days ago she might have wondered if it was so he could add weapons to his arsenal, but now she found herself trying to discipline a giddy kind of pleasure.

"I guess it's time for you to get going," she said, stamping down her wandering thoughts with an abrupt tone.

If Sam thought she was being rude, he gave no indication.

"I guess it probably is."

She likely only imagined the reluctance in his voice. But it didn't matter, she reminded herself. Despite what she'd been moved to share, it was still all business. It had to be. The fact that it was getting harder to remember that reinforced Claire's need to do so.

Her phone rang. It was Rachel, and for a moment she didn't know whether to welcome the distraction or worry about why her sister was calling.

Since Claire had become a mother, she often wondered if she would ever hear a phone ring or a knock at the door without her nerves asking "is everything okay?" But there could be any number of reasons for Rachel to make a quick call. It was probably nothing to be concerned about.

"Hi, Rachel," Claire answered.

"Claire, I'm so sorry to do this to you. I know you have a meeting at the shop today with Dorothy and Patrice Larsen to show them what you've been working on."

Okay, so it is something.

"What's going on?" Claire asked. "Is Maggie feeling worse?"

Maggie had been battling a stomach bug, and meeting or not, she would get home as fast as she could if her little girl needed her.

"No, she's not worse, but I can't take her to day care when she's contagious, and that's the issue."

"Okay…" Claire took a slow breath in and exhaled it.

"I thought about some of the neighbors, too," Rachel continued. "But I don't want them or any of their kids catching anything."

"What's going on, Rachel?" Claire asked.

"Well, do you remember a while back when I sent an application to one of the smaller art galleries in Regina to see if they needed someone to help with displays?"

Claire didn't specifically remember—Rachel went through times when she would get very determined and send out a flurry of applications—but she could hear the hope in her sister's voice.

"Did they offer you an interview?" She pushed aside her misgivings about what this would mean for her day. "Rach, that's great."

"They did," Rachel replied more quickly, encouraged by Claire's reaction. "They said they loved my résumé and they were sorry they'd taken so long to get back to me, but the person who makes those kinds of decisions actually lives in Toronto and comes to Regina about twice a year, so they try to arrange a day of interviews for him to do while he's here."

"And if your interview doesn't happen today," Claire said, reading between the lines, "you don't know if or when you'll get another chance."

"Yeah, exactly."

Claire tried to mingle a prayer in with the barrage of thoughts and options running through her head. She didn't want to ask the Larsens to reschedule because she had a pretty good idea of how Dorothy Larsen would react to that. But she wanted to make sure that this opportunity happened for Rachel. It was important to her future and it was what they both wanted, although it would open up a new box of complications.

"Bring Maggie here," she said firmly.

"Claire, are you sure?" Rachel asked.

"It's the only thing we can do." Claire's mind continued to race. "I can maybe figure out a way to make a place for her to lie down in the back and I can check on her. It'll be fine."

Please, God, help it all work out.

"Can I help with something?" Sam's quiet voice broke into the silence after Claire ended the call.

Claire's hand flew to her chest. Distracted by the phone call, she had managed to forget that Sam was there.

"I thought you were leaving," she gasped.

"I didn't mean to startle you..." His eyes studied her with concern. "But I'm glad I stayed, because it sounds like there's something going on. I didn't mean to eavesdrop, but I couldn't help hearing and wondered if there's anything I can do to make things easier for you."

Once in a while Claire did let herself indulge in the what-ifs of ways her life could be easier if she had a husband, so that these kinds of twists and turns in life would be mere hiccups that could be easily dealt with and not something that could potentially upend her entire day.

But that was not the reality of her life, so there wasn't much point in dwelling on things being different. It wasn't something she chose to pray about much, either. God had always cared for her and Maggie in one way or another, and if He seemed to think that she could manage as a single parent, who was she to argue?

But if she was going to pray about it, the last person she would have expected to be offered up as an answer was Sam Meyer. Surely, that couldn't be what God had in mind, even if there did seem to be moments of them bonding during the early hours at Love Blooms.

Still, she found herself explaining. "Rachel has a job interview that she can't miss, Maggie has a touch of the flu, so we have to keep her out of day care, and Dorothy and Patrice are coming here at eleven to see some of the ideas I've come up with."

"I could explain the situation to the Larsens," Sam suggested. "I'm sure they'd understand." But he sounded doubtful even as he was saying it.

"Absolutely not," Claire replied and shook her head. "I'm

sure Dorothy would have no desire to do business with someone who can't even organize her day."

Sam rubbed his chin with his thumb, looking thoughtful. "Would you be comfortable with me picking up Maggie?"

"You?" Claire asked. "Why would you do that?"

"Because," Sam said calmly, "it might be the best solution. Maggie knows me, we have a sickroom at the church, and I know my assistant wouldn't mind looking in on her."

Claire considered, thinking of Ann McFadden, the highly competent assistant to the clergy at the church, who was a trusted motherly figure, not only to her own family but also to the entire church. She would have no qualms about Maggie being under Ann's care for a few hours, and it was certainly a better alternative than making her sick daughter try to sleep in the back of the store and Claire feeling torn between her responsibilities, not that she wasn't already perpetually torn.

Yet, if she agreed, wouldn't it be breaking her determination to stay more distant from Sam?

Then again, hadn't she already closed some of that distance by sharing imaginings about bouquets for fairy-tale princesses?

He waited patiently for her answer, with nothing but compassion in his eyes.

I can do this for Maggie...and for Rachel.

She had not only her daughter's health and comfort to consider, but Rachel also finally had an opportunity that could lead to good things for her future.

"Would you phone Ann?" she asked. "So I know she doesn't mind?"

"Of course." Sam took out his phone, and Claire could tell from his end of the conversation that things were a go.

"Thank you," she said. "I'll call Rachel and let her know the situation. She'll need a few minutes to get Maggie ready."

Sam nodded. Then he reached out and gave Claire's wrist a little rub with his fingertips.

"Thank you for letting me help you, Claire."

"No, thank *you*, Sam."

Being abandoned by Maggie's father didn't make it easy to trust any man, but in that moment, she was grateful Sam was there to step in.

His presence was solid and offered security—even the smell of him, fresh detergent and a piney masculine soap, was comforting.

"Tell her I'll be there whenever she's ready for me," Sam said.

"I will," Claire said. "Thank you again."

"My pleasure. See, problem solved. Nothing to worry about."

Claire wanted to tell him that there was never a time when there was *nothing* to worry about, but she had to acknowledge that if there was anyone she would trust with Maggie, it was Sam.

Her little girl had never made any secret of her admiration for the pastor.

She called Rachel back and explained Sam's offer.

"And you're okay with this?" Rachel asked.

Claire assured her sister that she was, infusing her voice with as much confidence as she could.

"When does he want to stop by?" Rachel asked.

"Whenever is good for you."

"Okay, I'll give you a quick call back when Maggie is ready," Rachel said. She lowered her voice in a secretive way. "Sam is a really nice guy, isn't he?"

Claire murmured, "Mmm-hmm, yes," feeling her ears

flaming as if Sam could hear what Rachel said…and what the words insinuated.

She quickly brought the call to a close and turned to face Sam, hoping the chagrin didn't show on her face.

She didn't need or want to dwell on Rachel's implication that Sam's doing this meant he had a soft spot for her. No, he was simply a shepherd helping out one of his sheep.

"Is this okay?" Sam studied her face. "I saw you were having a dilemma and it was the first thing I could think of to help."

"I know that," Claire said, with maybe a touch too much emphasis. She softened her voice. "I do appreciate it."

Because Sam was right—she needed help.

She just wasn't all that used to getting it and she didn't want to need it.

The pastor drummed his fingers on his chin, looking thoughtful.

As if she needed anything else to draw her attention to the cleft in his chin.

"It's okay to ask for help, Claire," he said, like he could read her thoughts.

She took a deep breath, not knowing how to tell Sam how difficult it had always been for her to believe that— and how she especially hadn't wanted to need help from him, the person who, as far as she was concerned, still stood firmly in the way of her future goals.

But he was also kind. He listened to her and consistently demonstrated interest and respect. Her heart ached in confusion.

Even knowing it wouldn't change anything, it was nice to imagine, even for a moment, what it would be like to have that kind of partnership and support with nothing else standing in the way.

* * *

Sam leaned against the car and snapped Maggie's seat belt into place for her.

"How are you feeling?" he asked.

"As well as can be expected," Maggie said, exhaling a sigh.

Sam fought back a grin. He loved Maggie's quaint, mature way of speaking, even though—or maybe especially because—it always caught him a little off guard.

"It's not a long drive to the church," Sam said. "But you let me know if you need me to stop at any time."

"I have been given strict *in-struck-shuns,*" Maggie said, enunciating the word carefully, "not to throw up in your car."

Sam was jolted with amusement and pity at the same time.

"No big deal if it happens," he said. "It wouldn't be your fault. Tummy bugs can do that to a person. But why don't you hang on to this just in case." He handed her an extra-large take-out coffee cup that he'd been meaning to throw away, but hadn't got around to.

He suddenly remembered the way his own parents had reacted once when sitting in the back seat on a long drive on an especially hot summer day had done a number on his stomach. He closed his eyes briefly against the shame.

He would never, not in a million years, want to be responsible for making anyone feel that way and, for reasons he wasn't prepared to consider yet, especially not Claire Casey's daughter.

In many ways, Maggie Casey struck him as being quite different from her mother, although their mutual love radiated from both of them whenever he saw them together. He always loved the way Claire encouraged her daughter to be herself, always treating her questions and interest with respect.

He didn't think Maggie looked much like her mother, other than a little around the smile, which led him to the conclusion that she must resemble her father.

His stomach clenched in sudden anger at this person who had deserted this little girl and her lovely mother.

If he was ever blessed enough to have something like that in his life… But immediately a counter thought shoved its way in, telling him that was never going to happen.

Sam glanced at Maggie as he drove. She was quiet but didn't seem uncomfortable in any way. Her hat sported a dancing snowman—now, *that* was like Claire—and flattened her hair, making her face look thin and vulnerable.

Does your mom ever talk about me?

Okay, not a chance. He wasn't going to resort to acting like a grade-six boy, especially not with a four-year-old.

He could only imagine Claire's reaction if she had any sense that he even fleetingly considered what it might be like to have a relationship with her.

"I never showed up at Millie's door without flowers in my hands, did I, my dear?" Sam suddenly remembered his late maternal grandfather saying, with an adoring look at Sam's grandmother. "And look at us, all these years later."

Sam wasn't sure about the flowers, not with Claire being the expert and all, but he would definitely do something to show that she was treasured.

Not that any of that was ever going to happen, since his real goal was still to leave Living Skies for a bigger and better church on his desperate hunt to find something that might alleviate the constant bleakness.

"My auntie Rachel has a job interview," Maggie said,

speaking up again just as Sam was easing the car into his parking space at the church.

"I heard that." Sam turned off the engine and unsnapped his seat belt, then leaned over to do the same for Maggie. "I was glad to hear it, not only because it's great for your aunt, but also because I get to spend some extra time with you."

Maggie's eyes appraised him and Sam thought she was like her mother. She wasn't going to just accept a compliment at face value.

Then she nodded.

"Ready to go?" Sam asked. "How's your tummy doing?"

"It's okay," Maggie said. "I think tomorrow I might be ready to try some candy."

"Sounds like you're on the mend." After they'd gotten out of the car, Sam offered his hand and Maggie accepted it, which made his heart do an unfamiliar little tug. Together they began to walk toward the church.

"I sure hope Auntie Rachel gets that job," Maggie suddenly sighed. "It would be better for all of us."

Sam immediately knew she was mimicking the words and attitudes of the adults around her and wondered how many such conversations she had heard.

He had many questions, all of which he knew Claire would never forgive him for asking if she caught wind of it, which, of course, she would.

All the questions really boiled down to two—was she struggling financially more than anyone knew or that she would admit, and what was he prepared to do about it?

God, am I making a mistake being so persistent about my own wishes for the property?

But, no, he had a whole congregation to consider, an entire community, not just one woman whom he may or may not have been developing a crush on, and he still believed that his way could benefit so many more people.

But did it have to put Claire at a disadvantage?

The healing room at the church consisted of two beds—not fancy, but functional and comfortable enough, with quilts donated by the women's quilting club and blankets, books and a CD player with a selection of worship music donated by various others.

"Which bed would you like?" Sam asked Maggie.

She chose the one with a quilt of flowers—not a surprise there—and he showed her how to turn the small lamp on the table between the beds off and on. Then he explained about the call button that was slightly higher on the wall, and to buzz if she needed anything.

"Anything at all," Sam explained. "Except a pony. I can't promise I'll be able to bring one of those in."

A small smile tilted the corners of her mouth, but her eyes drooped with weariness. Getting up and dressed to go to the church had clearly worn her out.

"Do you want juice or anything before you tuck in?" Sam asked, helping her remove her boots and jacket.

She shook her head, rubbing her eyes. "I'm just sleepy."

"Okay…" He hesitated. "Remember the buzzer and Ann or I will come running."

"But not with a pony," Maggie murmured before her eyes closed all the way.

He laughed softly. "That's right—no pony."

He eased the door closed behind him. She was such a wise, funny little girl. He let himself ponder again for a moment what it would be like to have a wife and share laughter over the words and antics of their own child.

But what if the child was depressed and suffered like he did? He could never take that chance.

Sam swallowed and tried to turn his thoughts toward his workday, but he wondered if he should first call Claire and let her know the patient was safely tucked in.

No, he decided, she knew she could check in anytime and she was probably preparing for the Larsens.

He said a brief hello to Ann on the way to his office and told her that Maggie Casey was in the healing room.

In his office, he turned on his computer and attempted to make a start at some sermon notes. But thoughts of Claire and her meeting kept intruding. He knew how much she needed this, just as he knew how difficult Dorothy Larsen could be to please.

He prayed that the meeting would go well, for Maggie's healing and that Rachel would have a successful job interview.

If she could get a decent job, it might help take some of the pressure off Claire's shoulders.

He had caught wind that Rachel could be a bit flighty about her employment, or at least insistent that the job be something she believed would fulfill her, instead of viewing it as something she could contribute to help her sister and niece. Oh, he knew that she was a mostly willing baby-sitter, but he wondered if that was enough.

Still, Claire remained a loyal and supportive sister.

Rachel was doing her best, he hastily reminded himself, as they all were.

Although he returned to his sermon notes, it took every ounce of his willpower not to phone Claire.

The truth was that the more time he spent with Claire in her shop and the more he saw what she was able to do, the more invested he felt in her doing well and in wanting others to see her considerable creativity and talent and, in turn, to support her.

Plus, when she had shared her imaginings about saving fairy-tale kingdoms with her bouquets, his heart had opened in a way that almost frightened him, because he couldn't let himself care that much about one person's success, especially not when he had goals of his own that, if they came to fruition, would take him away from Living Skies—and from Claire and her life—anyway.

Maybe his early morning visits to Love Blooms had run their course.

With considerable effort, he ignored the knot of sadness this decision made in his throat, although it was a sadness that struck more deeply and in a completely different way than the chronic but mundane bleakness he always carried with him.

This pain had teeth.

Early in the afternoon, the call Sam had been waiting for finally came.

"How is she?" Claire asked almost before he could get his hello out.

"She's doing okay," Sam said in what he hoped was a reassuring tone. "Ann has checked on her a few times and says she's sleeping soundly. How was…?" Was it his place to ask? "How was your meeting with the Larsens?"

Claire's slight hesitation caused Sam to hold his breath.

"It was…okay."

"Only okay?" he asked, gentling his voice even as a rock of apprehension sank into his stomach.

"Dorothy had a lot of suggestions, and I mean a *lot*." Claire tried to chuckle, but the sound was rueful, and he could hear her effort not to sound disrespectful. "The truth is—" now all attempts at humor left her voice "—she didn't really like anything I showed her."

"What about Patrice?"

"I don't know. I think she might have, but it's so hard to figure out what she really thinks or wants."

Sam nodded, then realized she couldn't see him. "Yes, that's true," he said.

"I guess I don't need to tell you."

"I can talk to Dor—"

"No," Claire said, cutting him off. "She'll either end up wanting my flowers or not, but whatever she decides, I want to know I did it on my own."

Sam suppressed a sigh. Just as in the town meetings, he found himself filled with equal parts frustration and admiration for Claire's stubbornness and determination. It seemed that as soon as she allowed herself any vulnerability, as she had done earlier, she almost immediately regretted it.

"Have you heard from Rachel about how her interview went?" he asked. "Should I take Maggie back to your place when she wakes up?"

"I did get a text from Rachel," Claire said. "She sounded pretty upbeat, so hopefully that's a good sign. She asked if it was okay, since she was already out, if she could get a few errands done and won't be home until suppertime. You can bring Maggie by the store when she wakes up. I'll be fine now."

"Are you sure?"

Sam could practically sense Claire hardening herself through the phone, as if to make up for allowing herself to need something from him.

"Yes, I'm sure. She's my daughter and I'm used to handling things." The words *on my own* were unspoken.

You don't have to be.

But he couldn't say those words. Not when he really had nothing to offer her.

Later, when Sam and Maggie went back into the shop, Claire was engaged chatting with Grace Bishop, while Grace's adopted daughter, Gloria, a ten-year-old child with Down syndrome, happily browsed the colorful ribbons that were often used to adorn the bouquets.

Maggie hugged her mother, said hello to Grace and Gloria and, still sleepy, allowed Claire to lead her into the back room.

Grace Bishop was a well-respected physical therapist, an attractive and practical woman who now carried an extra glow about her ever since she had married the *Living Sky Chronicle*'s new editor and renowned photographer, John Bishop, and they'd adopted Gloria.

As a single woman, Grace had been the guardian to a foster child before marrying John Bishop and adopting Gloria, so she had an affinity for single parenthood and had always made it clear in the town meetings that she supported Claire's goals, and Sam was well aware that some of the other women did the same, whether they were single or married.

Claire returned and Sam lingered, listening to her interaction with Grace. Besides, he needed the opportunity to tell her he thought it best to discontinue coming to the shop in the morning.

But, really, he knew he stayed because he enjoyed watching her interactions with others.

Then something that struck him as odd caught his eye. Two boys that he recognized from his youth group, Evan Sinclair and Paul Beaudry, were also in the shop. They came out from behind a table filled with potted plants and headed in Gloria's direction.

Now, what interest would two teenage guys have in the flower shop?

Something told Sam to keep an eye on what they were

up to. Claire and Grace were still absorbed in their conversation.

Evan and Paul had always seemed like okay guys, as far as Sam could tell. They were both athletic and popular, but he'd never witnessed either of them be anything but inclusive with the kids at youth group who might have a harder time fitting in.

But ever since Claire had pointed out to him that sometimes bullying could go on in subtle ways that slid under the radar, he was afraid of missing something.

Of course, Claire had him second-guessing himself at every turn—a sensation that was more pleasant at some times than it was at others.

Now the boys were talking to Gloria and he couldn't quite make out what they were saying. Their expressions looked pleasant enough, but then Gloria's bright smile wavered uncertainly and her eyes squinted in confusion.

Sam couldn't stand watching any longer. He strode in their direction. "Hi there, guys," he said loudly. "Are you looking for some flowers?"

His voice drew Claire's attention and she hurried toward Gloria and the boys, planting her hands on her hips. Grace followed closely behind, holding worried questions in her eyes.

Evan smiled in the charming way he had, but he betrayed his nerves a bit by shifting his weight from one foot to the other.

"Oh, hey, Pastor Sam. I didn't know you were here. Paul and I were just, um…"

Here he looked at his friend, indicating that he should fill in the blanks, but Paul only smiled and didn't make eye contact. He clearly counted on Evan to take the lead.

Sam studied them both for a moment, intentionally remaining quiet to see what might stumble out of their mouths.

"We heard it was a nice place in here," Evan finally managed, while Paul nodded eagerly.

"Well, thank you for popping in to check it out," Sam said in an even tone. "Please make sure you tell everyone you know that it *is* a nice place. But I'm sure you need to be moving on now, am I right?"

The boys nodded. Sam could tell they weren't pleased with him but they weren't about to challenge him.

"Let me get the door for you," he said. He held it open and they hurriedly left the shop.

Grace was bent over Gloria, smoothing her bangs and speaking softly to her.

Over their heads, Claire's eyes met Sam's and he saw gratitude in hers.

Chapter Six

It almost frightened Claire how grateful she was that Sam had been there to spot a potential problem and to step up.

It made her ask herself why she was so reluctant to have him around and to accept his assistance with things, and the only answer she could come up with was that it was difficult for her to accept help from anyone. She hadn't exactly had the kinds of experiences in life that made that easy to do.

Sam really wasn't that difficult to have in the shop. As a matter of fact, his presence was a lot more soothing than she ever would have imagined when they disagreed at town-hall meetings.

He asked good questions, but he also knew when to stay quiet. Her worry that he would be critical and correcting had never come to fruition. Instead, she felt *seen* and appreciated.

He sees the flowers and he appreciates them, she quickly amended.

But right now there were other things to think about.

There should always be other things to think about than whether Sam Meyer liked her or not.

Claire thought about what had happened or what she suspected had been about to happen in her store and what

Sam had done to stop it. She didn't know what she would say or do if Maggie was ever the victim of bullies, but she was sure it wouldn't be pretty and she admired Grace's calming demeanor.

Sam stood close to Claire and she tried not to be distracted by the scent of lemony laundry detergent and a light, musky maleness that lingered underneath.

"Does that kind of thing happen often?" he asked grimly.

"You mean Gloria getting teased?" she asked, keeping her own voice low.

But Grace heard and threw a reassuring smile in their direction, then asked, "What do we say about people who tease us, Gloria?"

"We say, it's more about them than it is about me, and only God and I get to decide about me." As Gloria recited the words, her round face beamed proudly.

"That's exactly right." Grace leaned down and hugged her little girl.

"I hope Gloria doesn't get teased a lot," Sam said, after the little girl and her mother had exited the shop. "I would like to think that people here hold themselves to a lot higher standard than that."

"I hope so, too," Claire answered, frowning in concern. "I hadn't seen signs of it before today, but I guess you never know."

She wanted to talk to Sam about what had happened, particularly about some other thing she'd observed about Evan and Paul, but she didn't want to take advantage of his time.

"I don't want to keep you," she said. "I'm sure you're ready to be getting home. Thank you again for your help with Maggie today."

"I'm not in any rush," Sam said. "It was nice to spend time

with Maggie today," he added, "though I'm sorry it was because she wasn't feeling well. She's quite the girl, isn't she?"

Claire nodded, smiling. "That she is. Speaking of which, I'd better check on her and get ready to go home soon."

Sam nodded and seemed about to say something else but then didn't.

If Maggie was still sleeping, Claire thought, she could make some excuse to stay at the shop and to encourage Sam to stay so they could talk. But she really could *not* get in the habit of wanting him around. Her life was filled to the brim already. Maybe it wasn't filled with the things that she rarely allowed herself to dream of—like finding love and a partner to share her hopes and dreams, fears and sorrows—but it was definitely full.

Sam followed Claire to a table in the middle of the store, where she fiddled with one of the arrangements that the Larsens had rejected.

Claire focused on the chrysanthemums that symbolized fidelity, hope and joy, watching her hands work in an attempt to still the uneasiness that washed through her.

"I really do need to check on Maggie," she said. Then, almost despite herself, she added, "Wait here."

Her daughter had drifted off to sleep again and was breathing deep, even breaths, even emitting a tiny, whistling snore. Claire gazed at her, feeling an unfurling of the tension she'd carried around with her for days now. Sleep was good for Maggie and she had confidence now that her daughter would soon be over this flu.

Thank You, God.

"How's she doing?" Sam asked when Claire returned.

"Sleeping...snorning."

He smiled. "That's good."

"So about what happened here." Claire quickly steered

the conversation. She wasn't about to spend the time with Sam with them both getting gooey over her adorable daughter. That was a little more personal than she was comfortable with.

So why did her heart yearn to share those very emotions with someone?

"So, to add to the question you asked about Gloria getting teased," Claire said. "Most people are kind to her. I mean, it's not just kindness. I believe that most people genuinely like her. She's a likable kid."

"She is that, for sure." Sam nodded. "I think that little girl would give everyone she met some beams of sunshine if she could."

Claire nodded.

"But there's still a problem." Sam wasn't asking a question.

She nodded, breathing in the scent of the mums, hoping that it wouldn't always remind her now of rejection.

Evan and Paul were popular, well-liked kids, so what did their treatment of Gloria today mean?

Her instincts told her that what had happened today wasn't a one-off, despite their reputations of being friendly and inclusive.

But the question was, would Sam believe her, or believe only what he had personally witnessed about them?

She had started to enjoy not disagreeing with him at every turn. But he had also expressed appreciation for her straightforwardness, so maybe that was the way to go.

"I don't think the problem is with people in general being mean to Gloria," she said. "But I'm not sure I trust those boys. Something tells me this behavior didn't suddenly just surface today."

Sam didn't agree but at least appeared willing to listen.

"I can understand that people like them," Claire said. "They're both charming kids, and they can be friendly and helpful."

"But...?" Sam prompted.

"But they're young and human and imperfect like the rest of us. I don't know..." Claire shrugged a bit helplessly. "Maybe I shouldn't have said that. I can imagine there must be a lot of pressure involved in being school athletes and popular and having everyone expect certain things of you."

"Maybe so," Sam said, frowning. "But it doesn't excuse the way they treated Gloria, or excuse them if they've been hurting anyone else's feelings, either."

"I'm glad you were here when it happened," Claire said.

"You're glad I saw it because you didn't think I'd believe you if you tried to tell me," Sam observed.

It was strange to realize that often they were at odds not because they didn't understand each other, but because they did.

She opened her mouth to try to form some kind of reply, but before she could get it out, Sam said, "I want you to know that I've been thinking a lot about what happened that night at youth group when you dropped Troy off. I've been thinking about what you said, and much as I would like to believe that the kids in my youth group would never treat anyone badly, I have to admit that isn't true, especially not after what I've seen today."

Claire could see by the crease marring his brow and the shadows in his eyes that it wasn't easy for Sam to confess something like that. But she realized that it wasn't because he had been determined to prove her wrong, but because he wanted to believe the best about the youth he taught and shared with each week.

A feeling of wanting to reassure him rushed through

her. She wanted to tell him that he was doing a wonderful job and that he was surely touching lives.

But just as she was reaching for his hand, a cry sounded out from the back room.

She dropped her hand as suddenly as if something had burned them. "That's Maggie," she said, unnecessarily.

Was I going to hold his hand?

"You'd better go see what she wants," Sam said in a way that made Claire wonder if he had the same question.

In the back room, Maggie was sitting up, her hair in disarray, but already calmer when she saw her mother.

"I just forgot where I was for a minute," she explained in her charmingly adult way. Then, sounding distinctly more her age, she added, "I'm hungry. When are we going home?"

"You're hungry?" Claire leaned over and tickled Maggie gently under her armpits, basking in her daughter's giggles. "You must be feeling better."

"I am," Maggie confirmed.

"Did you have a nice time at the church?" Claire asked. Something about knowing that Sam was still out there in her store, waiting, made her strangely shy about asking the question.

"Uh-huh." Maggie gave a considered nod. "Of course, mostly I slept. Pastor Sam is very nice. If I had a dad, I'd want one like him."

Claire's hands froze on the straps of Maggie's boots.

Maggie never really asked about her father or talked about wanting one, and Claire had always reasoned that it was because she was used to the kind of life she had, so didn't consider other options.

Evidence that her daughter had considered what a different life might be like, one that could include a father figure, slammed into her, making her feel breathless for a second.

"Need help doing up my boots, Mommy?" Maggie offered.

"No, Magpie, thanks. I was just thinking." She finished the job. "There, all done—let's go. Hey, I have a surprise for you. Pastor Sam is still here. He waited to say hello to you."

She reasoned that it wasn't an untruth. Although she and Sam had other things to talk about, she also knew he would be happy to see Maggie up and doing much better before he went home.

Except now she thought maybe it was best if he did just say hello to Maggie and they didn't get chatting about other things, like the potential bullying in her store or even Dorothy Larsen's negative reaction to her floral efforts and what, if anything, she could do about it.

After Maggie's rather unnerving comment about the kind of father she might want, Claire began to think that it was more important than ever that she prove she could figure things out on her own.

As Maggie grew older, she would make her own decisions about relationships and Claire truly hoped she would find herself in a loving, happy marriage. But she also intended to show her daughter that there was nothing wrong with a woman standing on her own two feet.

Sam greeted Maggie with enthusiasm and, when he heard she was feeling better, treated her to a series of increasingly silly high fives.

Watching them, Claire struggled to gather her wits and to think clearly about her goals and what was important to her.

"We'd better get home, Maggie," she blurted out. The unexpected sharpness in her voice was enough to make them both pause and look at her.

She forced a smile. "I thought you said you were starving. I need to get you home and feed you."

She could read in Sam's eyes that he was also struggling with the abrupt change in direction, but his expression softened when he looked at Maggie.

"Getting something to eat sounds like a good idea," he said. "I'll be on my way and talk to you ladies soon."

He paused at the door, then turned to Claire and said, "We will continue our discussion later. Can I call you?"

With Maggie's avid eyes on her, Claire's cheeks and neck flushed pink.

"Umm, sure. Sounds good."

Sam had been awake far too long the night before trying to unravel the mystery that was Claire Casey and her advance-retreat approach to him.

Circumstances had prevented him from telling her he was ending his morning visits, and now he was no longer sure if that was best after all.

When his alarm clock went off, he had been unable to resist hitting the snooze button, promising himself—and God—he would make up the time.

"You're late, Pastor," Ann McFadden said as Sam tried to inconspicuously slip by her desk.

But there was no getting anything by her. Of course, that was only one of the things that made her such a wonderful assistant, and Sam knew they were blessed to have her.

He didn't let himself think about the fact that Ann would no longer be part of his church life, or his life in general, once he moved to a bigger church.

But then, the thought of unraveling what was really going on with the youth combined with a growing attachment to Claire and the people and passions in her life—despite his continuing efforts to fight it—caused him to ask himself if leaving really was the right solution.

Ann was a middle-aged Indigenous woman whose round face and medium-length, thick black hair shaved at least ten years from her actual age.

Come to think of it, Sam had no idea what her actual age was. He only knew that today wasn't the first time he wished she could be in charge of his life beyond church, but the urge for that was now particularly strong.

"Does Liam want to see me?" Sam asked, referring to the head pastor, Liam Barker.

"Not that I'm aware of."

"Okay… Just the way you said I was late, I thought someone must be looking for me."

Ann fixed him with a look. "And someone needs to be looking for you in order for you to be on time?"

"I didn't mean that." Sam scratched the back of his head. There were honestly times that he would rather face a room full of testy church-board members than this woman.

"Relax, Pastor." Ann's grin dimpled her cheeks. "I'm just giving you a hard time. But—" she pointed her finger at him "—you know I'm a stickler for punctuality. Plus, joking aside, it's not like you to be late. Do you mind me asking why?"

Ann could be on the intimidating side—despite her dimples and her soft-spoken voice—but she was also great to talk to, so Sam found himself telling her about the Larsen wedding, the early mornings at Love Blooms and even about Claire's misgivings over what might be going on within the youth group.

"Sounds to me like Claire Casey's opinion on things means quite a lot to you," Ann said when he took a breath.

Sam thought of protesting that observation, but, really, what was the point? Ann was sure to get to the heart of things.

"It does, though for the life of me, I don't know why." Sam paced back and forth a little in front of Ann's desk, while she watched him quietly, a slightly bemused expression on her face.

"I mean, I think she's a smart person and all," he said. "I think she's a great mother and she's so creative with her flowers, and the more I get to know her, the more I find her really delightful to be around."

Really delightful? Since when do I say things like "really delightful"?

To her credit, Ann kept a straight face.

"But when it comes right down to it—" he forced himself to sound brisk and full of business, definitely not a man who babbled on about someone's delightful company "—we really have different ways of looking at things."

"Do you think that takes away the possibility of being real friends?" Ann asked.

She opened the top drawer of her desk and busied herself lining up pens. Sam had observed in the past that she often made the effort to appear distracted when she was most interested in the answer to whatever question she had asked.

"I guess I don't see how a relationship can truly thrive over the years unless you have a lot of foundational things in common."

Ann pushed the desk drawer carefully shut.

"I don't recall asking about a relationship," she said, not smiling but with a distinct twinkle in her eyes. "But, okay, let's say that I was. Why are you so sure that a relationship with Claire wouldn't thrive?"

How had this conversation gotten so far off track? He certainly had no intention of discussing any kind of relationship with Claire Casey.

The back of his neck itched again. He wanted to say

something about needing to get to work, but somehow he still stood there, letting his church assistant plant thoughts in his head that he couldn't allow to be there, not when he coped with a hidden darkness that he refused to bring into anyone else's life.

"The funny thing is," Ann said, "we often like to think that we know what kind of person would be best for us and we really have no idea. Take my Bill." She smiled with a familiar fondness that wrenched Sam's heart with what he might be missing. "To start with, he's not Indigenous, as you know, so we had some cultural differences right here. He almost never stops talking, even when I'm trying to read, and no matter how many times I tell him I'm not interested, he won't stop trying to get me to go fishing with him. As if hearing his stories about it wasn't enough. But—" her dark eyes shone with a love that was deep and sure and true "—I never met a man with a bigger, more patient heart. There's nothing he wouldn't do to help someone out. He's a wonderful father to our children and every day he makes me want to be a better person. But if I'd gone after what I *thought* I was looking for, I might never have given Bill a chance," she concluded.

A kind of longing pushed at Sam's heart. But he pushed back. He wasn't ready to deal with any of that. He *couldn't* deal with any of that.

"You and Bill are one of the best couples I know," he said. "But the reason I'm wondering about Claire's opinion is because of a couple of things she's mentioned about the youth group."

Even with Ann's kind but shrewd eyes studying him, he tried to convey that was the only reason he was concerned about her opinion.

Yeah, right.

"Actually, Ann, I'd like to tell you about that. Do you have time?"

"I sure do, Pastor." Ann was suddenly all professional attentiveness.

"Let's sit in my office," Sam said. "I'll bring us coffee."

A short time later, he had outlined what had happened at the youth group the night Claire dropped off Troy Allen, and then, almost grimacing with discomfort, he recounted what he had witnessed at Claire's shop between the two popular boys and Gloria Bishop.

"Claire thinks there's definitely some kind of bullying going on," he concluded. "And she as much as said that she doesn't think that Paul and Evan are as nice as they pretend to be."

As he spoke the words, Sam wondered again if he could find it in himself to leave if an offer did come through. Was God reminding him of how much he was needed here?

Ann was silent for a moment. Then she took a sip of her coffee and leaned forward. "And you want to know if I think you should take Claire Casey's opinion into account?"

"I guess… I guess I'd be interested in hearing if you've noticed anything about any of the kids that you think I should know about."

Sam wouldn't say Claire's name again—not with Ann scrutinizing his face.

She sat back again. "I suppose I think that kids are human and humans are imperfect, so there's not a lot I could find out about any of them that would surprise me, or should surprise you, really."

"I suppose so," Sam murmured.

But he was pretty sure that the depths of his depression would surprise even the unflappable Ann McFadden.

It was strange. He had often thought that if anyone was going to be able to spot the cracks running through his facade, it would be Ann. But she continued to treat him as she always had.

"I should get back to work," Ann said, standing and pressing her palm against her lower back with a sigh. "*Some* of us have things to do."

"Yeah, yeah." Sam shook his head but smiled at her.

"You know what I think is a real surprise?" Ann said, pausing in his doorway.

"What's that?"

"Finding out something good about someone that you never expected, and realizing that they're meant to make a difference in your life."

She didn't say Claire's name, but Sam heard it in his mind—could almost see the woman herself filling up the space between them, with her beautiful eyes and shiny hair, and her strength and determination.

It was while he was trying, without much success, to concentrate on preparing for the next church-board meeting that Sam came up with the idea. There would be no more waiting, hoping that somehow someone would step forward and confess to bullying.

No, he was going to devote at least one evening of youth group to specifically tackle that subject, and he was going to ask Claire to help him.

He nodded with satisfaction and told himself that it had nothing to do with creating another reason to see her.

When he picked up his pen again, thoughts for a sermon seemed to flow a little bit easier, although he couldn't stop thinking about everything Ann had said.

Is God trying to tell me something?

After his supper of salmon, wild rice and green beans, Sam called Claire to share his idea about them tackling the potential youth group problem together.

"I was thinking we could do a kind of presentation to-gether."

"Together?" She sounded almost dumbfounded. "I've al-ready given you my thoughts on it and I'm glad you agree it's worth thinking about. But I'm not a teacher or a pub-lic speaker. Besides, I have Maggie to think about and I'm not going to just assume Rachel will be available. That's not fair to her."

"I'm sure we could make arrangements," Sam said. "If we coordinate it with other activities going on at the church, there's always childcare available."

He might be winging it, but he wasn't prepared to give up on the idea.

"I saw you with the youth that night at the church," Sam said. He closed his eyes and pictured it for a moment—Claire and her reindeer purse.

"The way the girls were crowding around you, they wanted to hear what you had to say, and you were so good with them."

"They were asking about my clothes and makeup," Claire said in a dry tone.

"Well...yes. But you were forming connections with them. I've noticed that you're good at that. Something I'm not as good at as I would like to be," he added, intention-ally blunt.

"Just a minute, please." She seemed to be talking to someone else at her home. A beat of silence, and then she said, "Okay, Magpie, I'll be there soon."

"It sounds like you're busy," Sam said. "But maybe we could talk about this another time?"

"It's fine," Claire said. "Maggie is just picking out her stories for tonight."

He resisted the urge to ask what books Maggie would

choose. There was so much he didn't know about the routines that made up Claire Casey's life, and he found himself wanting to.

He heard some more murmuring and then Claire's voice spoke more clearly into the phone.

"I appreciate you saying I'm good with people," she said. "But like I was saying, there's a big difference between making chitchat about clothes, or flowers, or whatever, and standing up before a group of youth and talking to them about a difficult subject. Besides—" a note of suspicion crept into her voice "—why aren't you asking Pastor Liam, or another youth pastor from a different church?"

Sam swallowed and he sought words to explain. But he didn't know how to tell her that, somehow, she made him believe that it was possible to be hopeful without getting into what a struggle that was and he wasn't ready for that.

But, meanwhile, Claire was still waiting for an answer.

"You are naturally good with the youth," Sam said. "They already like you and that's a huge start. But..." The ideas were forming as he was speaking. "You also mentioned that you had some struggles growing up because..."

He stopped talking, fervently wishing that he'd thought it through before he'd opened his mouth.

Claire finished the thought for him. She sounded calm—almost dangerously so.

"Because I was overweight I got picked on and you think that makes me the perfect person to talk to a bunch of kids who might also be picked on."

"That's not how I mean it, Claire," Sam said. "Not at all."

What is wrong with me?

It seemed like he couldn't go thirty seconds without messing things up with Claire, even though that was far from his intention.

Yes, he thought that her past experiences gave her sensitivity and might give her some insight into what some of the teens might be going through, but far more than that, he wanted them to be encouraged by the beautiful woman—inside and out—that she was now.

The truth was that he could probably call on any random person in the congregation or elsewhere and they would be able to share with the kids that growing up was tough and that not everyone was going to like you. They could share that sometimes life was just plain unfair, challenging and downright painful. The trouble was that, as their pastor, Sam knew that some of them still carried that attitude with them, never getting over their past burdens but instead lugging them along to clutter up present space.

Not Claire, though. Despite it all, even with the challenge of being a single mother with no involvement from Maggie's father, she seemed to face each day with gratitude.

That was what he wanted the young people to experience and learn from.

That's what I want to experience and learn from.

Now he just had to find the right words to convey as much to Claire.

"Look, Sam," Claire said. "I'm not sure how much longer I can be on the phone here. I have a little girl waiting for stories and bedtime."

He had better find the words and fast.

"I think you would be the perfect person to talk to the youth," he said, the words rushing out. "Not because of the person you were in the past but because of the person you are now. You're an overcomer, you're strong and you run your own business and bring beauty to everyone around you. *You* are beautiful."

Okay, so being beautiful wasn't a prerequisite for addressing the youth group, but he wasn't sorry he said it, not even when he heard Claire's small intake of breath.

Especially not then.

"I think you are the perfect person to give them hope," Sam concluded. "I'll let you go now, but please think about it."

"I'll give it some thought," Claire said and said a hurried goodbye.

Even though she said it like someone who just wanted to get off the phone, Sam chose to cling to her words. He'd had a taste of the kind of impact Claire Casey had on him and he believed in the impact she could make on others.

But his inner struggle continued, wondering if he dared stay in Living Skies and allow himself to benefit from her impact, or if he should continue in his quest to find another church.

Chapter Seven

Claire didn't want to think about Pastor Sam's request. Her plate was already full and in danger of spilling everywhere. She was a single mother, she had a business to run, she was still waiting for the Larsens' decision about the flowers and Rachel was still anxiously waiting for a job offer after her interview. Besides that, December was upon them and soon she would be striving to give Maggie a meaningful and joyous Christmas, using the resources she had to the best of her ability.

There was absolutely no way that she was going to stand in front of a youth group and chat with them like she was an expert on what they were going through.

Except, ever since Sam's phone call a couple of nights earlier, it was virtually all she thought about.

Thoughts of it followed her into her evening bath and couldn't be chased away by scented candles and inspirational music. The idea of it made her toss and turn her way into a restless sleep, and in the morning, danced across the pages of her devotional.

Lord, are You trying to tell me something?

Claire had always been fond of pro-and-con lists when she had a tough decision to make. She already knew that the cons list would have several things on it, which could be summed up by the sheer fact that she didn't think she could take on anything else.

The pros list had one item.

Maybe, with God's help, she could say something that someone needed to hear.

She promised herself that, one way or another, she would give her answer to Sam by Monday morning.

On Saturday, after she had closed Love Blooms for the remainder of the weekend—she never opened on Sundays—Claire decided to give Shirley Allen a call. She had been meaning to catch up with her. They had seen each other at book club, but that wasn't the right venue for the kind of conversation she hoped to have, and the book club was always on hiatus in December because everyone was so busy preparing for Christmas.

As she pressed Shirley's number into her phone, she prayed that God would guide what could prove to be a delicate conversation. But if she could determine if there really was something going on with Troy, it would help her make her decision on how she would answer Sam's request.

The winter sky was a deep gray, holding snow and seeming to signal change, one way or another.

She was still rapidly assessing the best approach as the phone rang, but being straightforward had always worked out best for her, so she would simply share what Sam had asked of her and see how Shirley reacted to it.

She had sought Shirley's advice before. Granted, it was mostly about real estate, but there was a what-happens-at-book-club-stays-at-book-club trust among the members.

"Hello?"

"Shirley, hi, it's Claire. I hope I'm not interrupting your supper."

"No, not at all," Shirley replied. "It's a nice surprise to hear from you. What's up?"

Claire's eyes scanned her living room as she gathered her thoughts. She could hear Rachel and Maggie's soft chatter and laughter in the kitchen. This decision, like all others, would be made by asking herself if it could ultimately benefit the people she cared about most.

But, somehow, now she was thinking about how agreeing to it might help Pastor Sam, though she wasn't ready to think about what that could mean.

She did know she liked seeing the warm light that came into his eyes when he was pleased with something.

"Claire…" Shirley's gentle voice was prodding her. "Did I lose you?"

"No, I'm here." She had to get to the point. She had used Maggie's bedtime routine as a way to get off the phone with Sam, but soon her daughter would be expecting her.

"Shirley, I actually called to get your thoughts on something."

"I'm all ears. What is it? Are you thinking of a change of locale, either personally or professionally?"

Claire could picture the other woman—she was tall and slim with short, always tidy-looking hair, which she meticulously kept dyed blond, and inquisitive brown eyes. She could almost see her leaning forward in her chair, maybe grabbing a notepad and pen to take notes.

"It actually has nothing to do with real estate," Claire said. She took a deep breath. "It has to do with something that Pastor Sam has asked me to do."

"He's finally asked you on a date!" Enthusiasm burst through the phone like sparks from a firecracker. "Of course, I think you should go. I'm so flattered that you thought of me as someone you can talk it over with."

A date? Where in the world did she get that idea from?

But maybe a better question was why she wasn't as appalled by the idea as she would have been a month ago.

She had better reel in that idea fast before the conversation—and her thoughts—went completely off the rails.

"He didn't ask me on a date, Shirley. This is about something else."

"Oh…" For a second that firecracker fizzled out, but then it sparked back to life again. "Well, I'm sure it's just a matter of time, if the way he looks at you is anything to go on."

Okay, she wasn't going to take time to ponder that…at least not now.

"He thinks that I can help him address something that he wants to talk to the youth group about," she quickly explained before Shirley could continue speculating.

"Flower arrangement?" Claire could practically feel Shirley's widening smile radiating through the phone. "That just sounds like an excuse to spend time with you."

"No." Claire refused to take the bait. It was already taking longer to get to the point than she had wanted. In the background, she could hear the first faint notes of giddiness creeping into Maggie's giggles, a sure sign that she was dangerously close to being overtired.

"He thinks I can address the youth on bullying," she said. Then, before Shirley could continue with her musings on Sam's possible romantic interest in her, she made herself be as blunt as possible, although saying the words caused an old yet very recent pain to rip through her.

"I told him that I'd experienced some bullying in school for being overweight, so he thought I might be someone who could talk to them about bullying—someone they might be able to relate to."

"Claire, is there a reason you're seeking my input on this?"

Shirley's voice had changed. It was still friendly—Realtor professional Shirley Allen was always friendly—but it held a wariness that hadn't been there before.

Now Claire wished that she and Shirley had nothing more to talk about than whether or not Pastor Sam Meyer wanted to take her on a date.

While Claire silently prayed to find a way to give the answer, Shirley provided the answer for her. "This is about Troy, isn't it?"

"Yes," Claire said, "it is, at least in part."

"He told me you were at the church the night things blew up in the youth group," Shirley said. "I've been meaning to ask you about it, but I just haven't found the right time. It's not something I wanted to bring up with the other women. It's just…you know—it's really hard."

"So Troy is being bullied?"

"I think so. He won't say much about it but he's changed." All brightness and energy left her voice. "He used to be pretty communicative for a teenage boy. At least, I always felt like I had a good idea of who his friends were, how classes were going, even the girls he liked. But lately he just shuts me out. It's like he wants to shut the whole world out."

Claire tried to imagine the difficulty of dealing with Maggie being bullied. Her heart wrenched with pain at the mere thought of it.

"I'm so sorry to hear that, Shirley," Claire said. "Troy is a nice kid. He doesn't deserve that."

"No one who's being bullied deserves it," Shirley said, sadness and frustration radiating from her voice.

"I know that," Claire hurried to reassure her.

"I know you're just trying to help," Shirley said after a

beat of silence. "Nothing that's happening is your fault and I don't mean to take it out on you."

"You're not, Shirley. I'm always here to listen. I just wish I could do more."

As Claire spoke the words, she became acutely aware of the opportunity that had been presented to her.

Her mind was made up. She would help Sam with the youth in any way that she could.

And she would not—would *not*—be thinking about what Shirley had said about the way he looked at her.

After the service on Sunday, Sam's eyes gravitated to Claire Casey, who looked to him like a lovely Christmas poinsettia. She was wearing a deep red wool dress, threaded through with shades of green.

Rachel wasn't with her this morning. Claire explained that she was a bit under the weather.

Maggie clung to her hand, smiling up at Sam in a way that made him wonder what it would be like to be a father… something he rarely allowed himself to consider.

He wouldn't want a sweet little girl like Maggie, or her mother, to have experienced him struggling just to get out of bed each morning.

On a learned, intellectual level, he believed God helped him, but, emotionally, there was often nothing but empty darkness.

Seeing Claire Casey, however, always gave him an inkling of hope, especially now that she'd told him of her decision to talk to the youth group.

"Did you enjoy Sunday school today?" he asked Maggie.

Maggie nodded and held out her artwork for him to admire.

"That's a beautiful rainbow," he said. Then he raised

his gaze to Maggie's mother and noticed the soft expression in her eyes.

Such beautiful eyes...

"We'll talk later about the youth group?" he suggested.

Instantly the softness was replaced by something else, but she nodded.

"Run and get yourself a cookie," she told Maggie. "I'll be right behind you."

Before she followed her daughter, she turned to Sam and said, "I just want you to know that this doesn't change anything. I want to be clear about that."

"What do you mean?" He was honestly befuddled in that moment.

"I'm agreeing to this because I think it's important to have open discussions about the impact of bullying and I want the world to be a better, safer place for Maggie, and for all kids, but I'm not backing down about the property."

Sam wasn't sure if she'd believe him if he told her that right then, the property they'd fought over was the last thing on his mind. So he simply nodded and said, "Understood."

Claire mingled easily with the crowd who snacked on coffee, tea and cookies that milled about in the church lobby every Sunday, unless there was a potluck being held in the fellowship hall downstairs. Then she would be likely to help in the kitchen, while still making sure that she got in plenty of visiting time.

She was so different from him. Making chitchat had always been difficult for him, somehow especially so while trying to balance a plate in one hand and a cup in the other.

Now Claire was talking to Dorothy and Patrice Larsen. They were all smiling, but since he knew their first meeting hadn't gone well, it sat uneasily with him.

Maybe Claire would be able to convince them otherwise, and was even doing so as he watched.

Of course, he couldn't just stand there watching Claire. Various members of the congregation came up to greet him and tell him that they had enjoyed his message to the children that morning.

"Even though the message is for children," Shirley Allen told him, "I always find something in it that I need for myself."

"Thank you, Shirley. I appreciate that," Sam said. "How are you doing?" He thought of Troy and something in the woman's eyes prompted him to ask the question and listen for a more than cursory answer.

But Shirley merely smiled and said, "I'm fine. Well, you know, busy as all get-out, but that's par for the course."

Sam nodded. "Yes, it seems to be that way, doesn't it? Take care—thank you again for your kind words."

It could be difficult, he knew, to get people to open up about what was really bothering them, or to even admit that something was.

But he could give a master class on hiding the truth, so who was he to judge?

It struck him that he would miss people like Shirley Allen—of course he would—even though he knew he could keep in touch with whomever he chose.

But escaping into a larger city and congregation had been his goal—his attempted solution to dealing with his depression—for so long that he couldn't stop wanting it now.

Yet more and more he'd been asking himself if he could.

But since Claire had made it clear that her goal had not changed, he saw no better options than to cling to his own.

He found himself seeking out Claire again. The coffee

crowd was thinning out and a few of the faithful regulars were starting to gather cups, glasses and plates and carry them into the kitchen. Claire was helping with that, Maggie by her side, carefully holding two half-empty glasses of juice, clearly proud to be helping.

He couldn't exactly follow her into the kitchen and ask what she and the Larsens had talked about. Yet he couldn't escape an urge to protect her from whatever hurtful things might be coming her way.

He said goodbye to the few stragglers, thanking them for their encouraging words and trying not to make it too obvious that he was keeping an eye out for someone. He didn't think he'd seen Claire leave.

When she came out of the kitchen, their eyes met and his heart tangled in a knot composed of the unknown and a deep, profound familiarity.

She took a few steps in his direction. Then the toe of one of the shoes she'd switched to on arrival caught on the corner of the carpet and she stumbled forward.

Maggie blurted out, "Mommy!" and made a grabbing motion at Claire's arm.

Sam gasped and started to run forward, but she wavered a bit, then righted herself. There was a beat of silence… Then she threw back her head and laughed uproariously.

When Sam thought at all about marriage, he always assumed he would eventually marry someone much like his mother. But now a thought as clear and sharp as a shard of glass pierced through his mind.

Someone like Claire would be much better for me.

But he couldn't let himself think that way. Claire wasn't going to rescue him from the things he was struggling with—no one was—and it wouldn't be fair to put that burden on her.

"Are you okay?" he asked. Even though she was standing and seemed perfectly okay, he still reached out and cupped her elbow as if to steady her.

Her skin was soft and warm; she smelled like the enticing mingling of Christmas oranges and sugar cookies.

And her gaze fixed on his hand like she'd never seen one before. Maggie watched, too, but didn't seem to mind.

Sam withdrew his hand, forcing himself not to show his reluctance to do so.

"I should know better than to wear these shoes," Claire said. "They're built for prettiness more than practicality."

"No, no, you're not the only one who's tripped on that carpet," Sam said. "We need to do something about that. I like your shoes."

Have I ever, in my entire life, told a woman that I like her footwear?

Claire's mouth quirk showed that she was wondering the same thing.

"Let's get going, Magpie," she said, after a moment. "See how Auntie Rachel is doing."

Sam began to walk with them toward the front door of the church. He just wasn't able to let Claire leave without finding out something about her conversation with the Larsens.

"I saw you talking to Dorothy and Patrice. Were you... okay with the conversation?"

Claire stopped walking and turned to face him. "What would make you ask that?"

But her expression wasn't defensive. It was more like what the question really meant was "how did you know to ask that?"

"I don't honestly know," Sam confessed. "I just saw something in your face. I know how much passion you put into your work and how difficult it must be when people don't appreciate it…"

His voice trailed off. He probably sounded like a complete idiot. He wished now that he hadn't started the conversation, not with Maggie there waiting and listening so intently.

But Claire was looking at him with a shy sort of glow in her eyes, as if she had been given a gift she treasured, without knowing that she wanted it.

"It was about the flower arrangements," she confirmed. "They want to meet again and see if I'm able to incorporate some of their suggestions."

She sounded grateful to have been offered another chance, but somehow, this displeased Sam. Claire should be given all the chances in the world and they should be grateful for her gifts.

"Are you kidding me?" The words exploded out of his mouth. "Your work is amazing."

Okay, so he wasn't acting in a very pastor-like way and was taking this way too personally on Claire's behalf.

Claire half laughed, half frowned. "I appreciate your support, but if they don't see it that way, I'll just have to try harder."

"I could…" Sam hesitated.

"What?" Claire asked, with the look of someone who both didn't want to need help but knew that she did.

"I could talk to Dorothy and put in a good word for you."

"I'm sure I'll be able to get it figured out," Claire said, with a slightly uneasy expression. She bent down to Maggie and fiddled with the zipper on her purple coat. Then she helped her daughter with her boots and exchanged her shoes for her more practical winter boots.

"Think of it as a trade-off," Sam urged. "You're helping me with the youth, so I'm more than happy to help you with the Larsens in any way that I can."

"Well, if you put it that way, thank you," Claire said. "I would never have thought of the two us as a team, but I guess, as they say, 'God works in mysterious ways.' Let's go home and make some lunch," she said, addressing Maggie again.

That had gone better than Sam had expected, but the funny thing was that he had no doubt that the next time they were at a town-council meeting together, they still wouldn't agree on anything.

Somehow, that just made him like her more, even though it also meant he was no longer sure of what he wanted.

"I want you to know that I trust you, Sam," Claire said suddenly, as they stood in the open door of the church, with the snap of winter air surrounding them. "There may not be a lot we agree on, but I know that if you say you'll help me with this, you will."

Smiling, Sam shook her hand, and warmth rushed through him like coming to a place he hadn't known he wanted to reach but felt like home.

Maybe later—much later—he would ask himself if he would ever consider trusting Claire in turn. Trusting her enough to share his struggles with depression.

In the meantime, he would do his best to not let his secret reveal itself, because, despite everything standing in the way, he wanted Claire Casey in his life in whatever way she could be.

Chapter Eight

Opening the door of their condo, Claire called out, "Hey, Rachel, we're home."

"In the kitchen," Rachel answered, her voice a croak. "Just making some tea."

"I can make that for you," Claire said worriedly. "You sound rough."

A rush of guilt shot through her as she realized that she hadn't given her sister a thought since church, not since Sam's warm and steadying hand had cupped her elbow to steady her when the carpet tripped her. She'd been too busy trying to figure out where the line blurred between letting him help her and forgetting she had to keep her eyes on what she wanted.

"I actually feel better than I sound," Rachel said. "How was church?"

"It was good," Claire answered, wondering why she felt like she was keeping a secret from her sister. "Maggie, why don't you show Auntie Rachel your Sunday-school art while I make lunch."

She was particularly grateful to have some time to pray and process through things as she put together sandwiches of honey ham and Havarti cheese on rye bread, and simmered a pot of tomato soup to go with them.

She had prepared herself for the Larsens to be discerning, even somewhat critical, and she had never shied away from a challenge. She'd had challenging customers before, but with communication and her innate confidence in her own work, she always managed to put together something that the customer was satisfied with, and that she was proud to have the Love Blooms name attached to.

But out of respect for the relationship he had with them, she would never have complained about them to Sam.

How would she say—even if it was something he already knew—that Patrice was so under her mother's thumb that she seemed to have no idea what she really wanted? While Dorothy was intent on finding something wrong without successfully communicating what her expectations were.

Claire's thoughts churned as she gave the soup a stir, turned the burner off and carefully transferred the contents into bowls to cool down.

As she had told Sam earlier, she had anticipated problems with him, not them. She probably shouldn't have said that, Claire mused. Her mother often told her that she was too blunt with people, not too subtly implying that it might be one of the reasons why men often weren't romantic about her.

Sam thinks I'm beautiful.

He had offered to help her and he did seem able to be objective about the Larsens.

She thought about all the times recently that he had complimented her and offered his help. Was it possible that he was interested in her?

Then she reminded herself that he was a pastor and it was probably in the job description, or at least strongly implied, that a pastor should be interested in and helpful to everyone, especially those in his congregation.

Too bad telling herself that didn't take away the shock of awareness that ran through her when he'd cupped her elbow after her tripping incident.

Would he have done that with anyone?

But why should she care? They were still the people who bickered constantly, and whatever this was, it was definitely just an interlude to their next disagreement.

So why did thinking about their next "quarrel" make her smile?

"What are you smiling about?"

Claire jumped a little and her hand knocked one of the plates on the counter, sending it and the sandwich tumbling onto the floor.

Thankfully, the plate didn't break.

"Jumpy," Rachel observed, carrying her cup of tea to the kitchen table and sitting down.

"You caught me daydreaming." Claire crouched to pick up the plate and sandwich, the latter of which she discarded into the garbage. She put the plate in the sink and washed her hands.

"You can have this one—" she indicated the other sandwich on the counter "—and soup's ready. It'll just take a minute for me to make another sandwich."

But Rachel leaned her elbows on the counter and rested her chin in her hands, looking inquisitively at Claire.

"What *were* you smiling about?" she persisted. "You were in another world there for a minute."

Claire was glad that Maggie had left the kitchen to change out of her church clothes and wash her hands for lunch. The last thing she needed right now was her daughter hearing Rachel's questions and offering her own opinion on the interactions between her mother and the pastor.

Most of the time she enjoyed Maggie's old-for-her-years observations, but now was not one of those times.

"Oh, just about something in church today," Claire said, turning away from Rachel to get the sandwich ingredients out of the fridge again, glad to have a reason to escape her sister's scrutinizing gaze.

Rachel was an astute observer and often saw things that Claire would have rather kept hidden from her.

It wasn't exactly a lie, she defended herself. She had been thinking about Sam and he was part of church.

But then again, she hadn't said she was thinking of *someone* at church.

"I'm glad that you're starting to feel better," Claire said, changing the subject. She would sort out her feelings, or at least attempt to, in her quiet time with God, either later that evening or early in the morning. It was her own fault that she had wasted the few quiet moments she had making lunch to speculate on exactly what Pastor Sam meant by helping her instead of thinking through more important things, like how she could please Dorothy and Patrice Larsen without losing her own creativity in the process.

Maggie returned to the kitchen and they all gathered at the table with their soup and sandwiches.

Claire asked the blessing and then there was silence for a few minutes while they soothed their hungry stomachs with the first few bites of lunch.

Claire spooned a savory spoonful of tomato soup into her mouth, her thoughts returning to her flower arrangements. She was always open to suggestions, but it was difficult when she'd already put great effort into creating something she thought would please someone and her efforts were rejected.

I wonder what ideas Sam has.

She bit almost angrily into her sandwich. Did thoughts of him have to intrude into every area of her life? It wasn't like she had no one else she could talk to.

"Rach, I need your thoughts on something."

Her sister frowned and picked off the corner of a crust of bread before looking up. She asked, "What about?"

"You know I'm doing flowers for the Larsen wedding?"

"Yeah, that's pretty hard to miss," Rachel teased.

"It's not going all that well, to tell you the truth. They don't like any of my ideas so far."

Rachel tilted her head and pursed her lips. "I don't know them well, but Dorothy strikes me as very opinionated and I don't think that Patrice ever stands up to her."

"What does *o-pin-yin-ated* mean?" Maggie asked, carefully sounding out the word.

"It means that someone feels very strongly about something," Rachel answered her.

"Sam says that they are just people who know what they want," Claire said.

The instant his name was out of her mouth, she regretted it. She'd done exactly what she was trying to avoid.

"Sam as in Pastor Sam?"

"Of course." Claire strove for an airy tone, which she knew she wasn't even close to pulling off. "Who else would I be talking about?"

"I didn't realize the two of you had gotten close," Rachel said, with a tone that said she approved.

"We haven't." Claire heard the defensiveness in her voice. This wasn't the direction she wanted the conversation to go in.

"You should be friends with him, Mommy," Maggie announced. "Pastor Sam is nice."

Why had she mentioned his name? She had to get the conversation back on track again.

"That's too bad," Rachel said, spooning up the last of her soup. "Because like I've said, I can tell that he likes you."

"He's a pastor and it's his job to be good to the people in his congregation," Claire insisted, sliding a pointed look in Maggie's direction.

Maggie took the last bite of her sandwich, thoughtfully chewed and swallowed, but Claire could tell she was paying attention.

Okay, she thought, maybe she hadn't picked the best time to ask for Rachel's input. She didn't want Maggie hearing negative thoughts about others.

Rachel finished her sandwich and pushed her plate away, a habit she'd had since she was a child to indicate that she was done.

"There are cookies for dessert," Claire offered. "They're store-bought," she added needlessly, because everyone knew her talents didn't lie in baked goods.

Maggie said yes but Rachel declined and began to clear the table, carrying dishes to the sink.

After Maggie finished her cookie, Claire got her settled with a picture book in the living room and returned to help Rachel with the clearing and washing dishes.

"I haven't heard you say anything about the property for a little while," Rachel mused as she dried a plate. "You still want to expand, don't you? I'd love a chance to show my work somewhere. I have more stationery and card designs that I want to show you."

"I'd love to see them," Claire said. "I haven't said much because I've been focused on the Larsen wedding and there hasn't really been anything to update. But, of course, I still want it. Don't forget, though," she added, "you're still wait-ing to hear from your job interview."

Rachel shrugged a bit despondently. "I can't help feeling that if they wanted me, I would know by now."

"Don't think that way," Claire urged. "Sometimes these things just take longer than we think. We'll keep praying about it."

But uneasiness settled over Claire. What if neither of them got what they needed or wanted?

Sam's face swam into her mind and she realized that she wasn't completely sure what she wanted anymore.

"I suppose," Rachel said, putting the last bowl away in the cupboard. "I'll be in my room if you need me for any-thing."

Claire stayed where she was and asked God, *Please, is there a way this can work out for all of us?*

She knew that she was now including Sam in the "us."

But there didn't seem to be an easy answer for that ques-tion, or for what she needed to do about the Larsen wed-ding flowers.

The only thing she knew was how confused she was.

When Wednesday night youth group rolled around, Sam was looking forward to seeing Claire, perhaps more than he should be, and was relieved when he spotted her.

It wasn't that he thought she was the type to break her promises—just the opposite—but he was sure that if Mag-gie hadn't been with her at church on Sunday, she would have had more to say to him about the Larsens' reaction to her flower arrangements and his offer to help. He could tell that neither of those things had sat easily on her shoulders.

Had she sensed how connected he felt to her when he

held her arm to help her right herself on the errant carpet and had that totally scared her away?

He knew it had scared him.

He didn't have the emotional health to share as deeply and warmly as a beautiful and caring woman like Claire deserved.

For some reason, trying to sort through all of this had made him worry that Claire would change her mind and not come, but here she was, though no Maggie in sight.

"Where's Maggie?" Sam asked her.

"Rachel said she wasn't doing anything tonight and that Maggie might as well stay home with her."

Sam heard a bite of worry in her voice and wondered if Rachel was sinking into the unemployment doldrums, as she'd been known to do before.

He knew that Claire never wanted to treat her sister as a built-in babysitter, but, instead, genuinely wanted Rachel to find fulfillment in her own life.

Claire was dressed in a navy blue dress with long sleeves and a skirt that swirled becomingly around her strong legs. For a Claire-like touch of whimsy, tiny snowmen held hands around the cuffs of the sleeves.

He longed to tell her how lovely she looked—how lovely she always looked.

Help me here, please, Lord.

He needed to be able to focus on the task at hand, not wallow in a crush—if that was what it was—that he couldn't and wouldn't do anything about.

The kids wouldn't arrive for another twenty minutes or so. Somehow, the pastor in him took over.

"We might as well go into the fellowship room and you can have a look at how things are set up," he said.

Claire followed him in and studied the room.

After a moment, she said, "Let's put the chairs in a circle and I'll just sit with the kids. I don't want to be up there like I'm giving a big speech or something."

"Absolutely," Sam agreed quickly. "We can do that."

They worked quietly together moving the chairs into a circle. Sam checked the time.

"Ah, we didn't find the time to go over what you planned to say tonight," he said.

"Did I need to get your approval?" Claire's tone was light but her expression was determined.

"Of course not," Sam said, trying not to be distracted by the pink flush on her cheeks and the spark in her striking eyes. "But I could offer some tips. Speaking in front of people isn't easy, even if you're used to it."

"Well, that's why I don't plan on speaking in front of them." Claire pointed to the chairs and her grin broke the tension of the moment.

Then, humor replaced by a kind of calm trust, she added, "I've prayed that God will help me find the right words."

Something lodged in Sam's throat. If only he could have that kind of simple trust, but his depression didn't allow him to.

Forgive me…

"That's a good idea," he said, managing a reply.

For the remaining time before the youth arrived, they kept themselves busy preparing the cookies and lemonade that would be served following the discussion. If Claire was nervous, she didn't show it. She had shown up and she was trusting God.

He couldn't remember when he'd ever admired someone so much.

Forty-five minutes later, his admiration had only grown deeper and he promised himself he would have a heartfelt talk with his Heavenly Father that night. There was simply something about Claire that drew people to her. Sitting in the circle of chairs, the youth treated her like one of their own.

He was there as a facilitator and adviser as needed, but it didn't take long to realize that he could stand back and watch how things unfolded.

It was humbling to realize how little he really knew about the kids that he saw at least twice a week. Oh, they liked him fine, at least he'd never had any indication otherwise, but it was dawning on him, as it had been since the evening that Claire had dropped off Troy Allen, that they didn't really open up to him.

In unadorned words, without overdramatizing, Claire spoke about her own experiences in high school as an overweight girl and how her strong faith helped her realize that even though she might never fit in, God would help her find her own way to stand out.

"Every single day," she said earnestly, "when I open my flower shop, I am so grateful that God allows me to express myself and my creativity in a way that's meaningful to me." She paused and her gaze swept the circle of young faces around her.

"Every single one of you has some kind of gift to share," she said. "A way to express yourself that makes you wholly you. You might not even know what it is yet, or maybe you know and you're not sharing because you think others won't get it. But trust me, if it's something God has given you, He'll make sure you find the best way possible to use it, and once you understand what your real strengths are, what others think and say about you won't matter nearly as much. I know that some of you—maybe most of you— are struggling to believe that right now, but it's the truth."

Sam observed the teens' gazes locked on Claire with an intensity he hadn't experienced from them.

"I'm making it sound like it should be easy," Claire continued. "I know that it's not. I still get my feelings hurt." She wasn't seeking pity—was just being truthful.

Sam had always admired Claire's honesty, but now he simply wanted to gather her into his arms and promise that he would never let anything or anyone hurt her again.

But he was hardly in the position to make that kind of promise, and besides, wouldn't the youth *love* that?

Her openness and vulnerability encouraged others to open up and it was an eye-opening experience.

Girls who conducted themselves with a confidence that sometimes hovered dangerously close to arrogance confessed that there were times that they felt they didn't measure up. One even said, in a soft voice, while she studied her feet, "I've teased people for looking different or not fitting in. I'm not going to do that anymore."

The boys were not as forthcoming with their feelings, but Sam thought their silence was telling. They weren't making jokes or trying to gloss over anything.

But he had not seen Jason, the boy from another town, since his discouraging visit to youth group, and he noted that Evan Sinclair and Paul Beaudry were conspicuously absent, which was too bad because they could have benefited from the message.

Then again, realistically, if they were behind much of the bullying, as Claire suspected, they might not care.

Troy Allen was missing as well.

As much as Sam enjoyed seeing a deeper side to the young people he welcomed each week, his stomach fluttered with anticipation as the evening drew to a close. He really wanted to talk to Claire and prayed that she wouldn't find a way to slip out before he had the opportunity.

After the last of them had thanked Claire and departed, he spoke quickly.

"Do you have a minute?"

"Maybe just a minute."

Now that he had her attention, he wasn't entirely sure what he wanted to say.

"You were amazing tonight."

Amazing—it was a word sweet and strange on his tongue, but he wanted Claire to know that he thought so.

"I just talked about my own experiences." Claire was striving for nonchalance, but the way she chewed her lower lip showed that she was more impacted by his remark than she wanted to let on.

"I can only pray I made some kind of positive impact," she said, "though I'm guessing they're still a bit young to really believe they won't always care so much about what others think of them."

Sam was silent as her words struck him deep. He was years beyond being a teenager, but he knew he still cared far too much about other people's opinions.

Why else would he keep his depression wrapped around him like a dark secret?

"I can't believe we're into December already," Sam commented before the silence grew uncomfortable. "It will be time to start getting the church decorated soon. Has Maggie said what she wants for Christmas?"

"Books," Claire said. "Always books and maybe a game that teaches her something. Those are her words, by the way."

Her fond smile added a beautiful light to her face and it made Sam's heart ache a little with the sudden wish that he could somehow share in the parent-child bond.

He really had to buckle down and commit to making his move to a bigger city and church early in the New Year, before he completely talked himself out of it. He knew it wasn't the best idea to want to involve himself more in Claire's life, even if she wanted him to, which she definitely did not.

Which meant he didn't quite understand himself when he asked, "Will Maggie be waiting up for you? Is there any possibility I could buy you a decaf coffee or a tea? Or what about hot chocolate?"

She could not have looked any more surprised at the suggestion, and for a moment, Sam prepared his ego to take a hit.

But then he thought of the vulnerabilities she had shared with such directness and dignity, and sensed that being chosen still surprised her. It didn't help, either, that Maggie's father had not bothered to stick around.

Suddenly, he didn't want to be a date or a counselor. He simply wanted to be a friend.

And he could also use a friend. If Claire could share so openly about difficult things, maybe he could, too.

Chapter Nine

Claire considered Sam's offer. She could use getting home to Maggie as an excuse, but knew that her daughter would be tucked in and that Rachel probably wouldn't mind if the evening was extended just a bit longer.

What concerned her was how much she wanted to go, how her heart had leaped at the invitation. She didn't ever want to be one of those women who started letting her imagination run wild when someone was simply being kind, as, of course, pastors were supposed to be.

Men didn't choose her, not romantically and not for the long term. She'd accepted that, and occasionally had a good, cleansing cry about it, and then gotten on with life.

It didn't make any sense at all that a casual offer from her property nemesis would cause her to wonder, if even for a moment, if she should open her heart up to possibilities.

It didn't help, either, that Sam's comforting smells of soap and mint and, somehow, books wafted gently in her direction as he stood close, waiting for her answer.

It was enough to make her want to bury her face in his shirt and stay there.

Even as she was offering a prayer for God's help in making the best decision, she knew she wanted to go.

"I'll just give Rachel a quick call," Claire said, and the

light in Sam's eyes made her hopeful for a moment that the invitation contained more than kindness.

Despite their disagreements over property and the emotional walls she always kept up after being picked on in school and abandoned by Maggie's father, she liked Sam. More than that, she trusted him.

Murphy's Restaurant, a comfortable, down-to-earth kind of place, known for its homestyle recipes and baking, did a rollicking business for breakfast, lunch and supper, and was known to fill up again in the evenings when people were looking for a treat after their other activities.

When Claire and Sam arrived, however, the restaurant was in a lull, with a few couples scattered at tables here and there.

Claire swallowed and rubbed the back of her neck.

We're not here on a date, she told herself. *There's nothing to be nervous about.*

But did she wish they were?

"Looks like it's date night," Sam remarked, causing her to inwardly squirm a little as his words too closely echoed her musing. But he surveyed the restaurant with an expression of mild interest.

"Hey, Pastor Sam," Renee Pierce, who was the receptionist at the Elmview Physical Therapy clinic, where Grace Bishop worked, called out and waved. Her bottle-assisted red hair was brighter than ever and the young man with her, whom Claire didn't recognize, looked a bit like a besotted owl, behind a pair of oversize glasses.

A giggle exploded out of her and she quickly snapped her mouth shut.

"Looks like love is in the air," Sam said quietly. He didn't even look at her, but something about the way he said it told

Claire that he had noticed what she had and also found it amusing.

It reassured her.

Renee's greeting was the first of many and a reminder that, while no one was ever exactly inconspicuous when coming into Living Skies' favorite restaurant, even during a slow time, it was even less so if you were in the company of a popular youth pastor.

Because Sam was popular, despite his reserved nature, there was something compelling about him…something that Claire was becoming increasingly aware of.

People greeted Claire, too, of course. With her flower shop and tendency to be outspoken, she was also well-known in the town.

But it hit her like a sudden punch to the gut in an unfair fight that she still often felt like a stranger, in part because of the emotional scars of being unpopular in high school, and in part because her daily responsibilities didn't allow her to partake in many things. Not that she regretted having Maggie. She might have regretted how it came about— how she let her longing to be noticed, to be loved, lead her into temptation. But even through that, God knew what He was doing, because Maggie was the best part of her life.

Still, there were times she wished she had time to explore more activities and friendships.

Michelle waved at them and said, "Sit anywhere. Do you need menus?"

Sam looked questioningly at her and Claire shook her head.

"I think we'll just be getting a couple of decaf coffees," Sam said.

"Sure thing."

Sam passed the tables that were occupied and chose one

by the windows, out of hearing distance. Claire was aware of the speculative eyes that followed them and wondered how many questions she would be fielding tomorrow about her "date" with Pastor Sam.

Michelle brought over a tray with two glasses of water with ice, a coffee carafe and two cups, along with cream and sugar. She set a glass of water in front of each of them and filled their mugs with coffee.

"Just wave me down if you decide you want anything else," she said.

"We will," Sam said. "Thanks, Michelle."

"Yes, thank you," Claire echoed.

"I just wanted to say again that you did such a wonderful job tonight," Sam said, as soon as Michelle stepped away.

Claire picked up her glass of water and swirled the ice, while her stomach swirled, too.

He's just being nice. You're not on a date.

Sam folded his arms on the table and leaned forward slightly. "When I heard you share so openly with the youth tonight, it got me thinking that I need to start doing a better job of being open and honest in my own life. Despite our many differences—" Sam's mouth quirked into a grin that warmed Claire throughout "—I've always thought of you as someone I could fully trust."

The words settled over Claire like being wrapped in her coziest blanket.

"Which is why…" Sam paused and a flicker of nervousness passed over his face as he tapped two fingers in a light, seemingly unaware gesture on the table. "There is something I think I want to talk to you about."

"Talk to me?" Claire repeated. Sam's hazel eyes studied hers as if he was hoping to find answers in them.

"Yes… I think I do. This isn't something I've ever really talked about with anyone."

Claire couldn't imagine what Sam could possibly want to talk to her about. He was the thorn in her side at town meetings, the man who stood in the way of her getting the property she wanted. Yet he was also unfailingly kind to the people around him, he was fair and he kept offering his help to her, whether or not she was willing to receive it.

There was only one way to respond that she knew she could live with. "I'm listening."

Sam took in a deep breath, then exhaled. His fingers drummed faster, then suddenly stilled. "I guess there's not a fancy way to say this. I'm depressed."

The words were the last thing Claire had expected to hear—although she couldn't have said what she might have expected, either.

But it wasn't hard to realize that even a pastor could have challenges, or especially a pastor. Maybe he was struggling with the week's sermon or had received some negative feedback.

"It's not about anything in particular that's happened or is going on in my life," Sam said, as if he had anticipated her thought process. "I am clinically depressed. It's something I have to live with and deal with every day, every moment of my life."

Claire curled her hand around her coffee mug, lifted it and breathed in its rich aroma before taking a sip, giving herself time to reply—giving herself time to pray.

She couldn't pretend that Sam's revelation hadn't shaken her. Not because she thought less of him as a pastor or a human being—she did not—but because she thought she'd had this man pretty well figured out, and now she realized that she'd had absolutely no clue.

Sam sipped his own coffee, his eyes anxious over the rim. She had to say something before he regretted choosing her to be the person he opened up to.

He chose me.

The first thing that came out was a question. "Why don't you tell people?"

Sam lowered his mug and returned with a question of his own. "Who wants to hear that about their pastor?" He closed his eyes as if something pained him, then opened them again.

"I guess I don't want them thinking that it means I don't have faith."

"That's ridiculous," Claire blurted out, and Sam blinked in surprise.

"No, no, I don't mean you're ridiculous," she quickly reassured him. "I mean, if people think that being depressed means you don't believe, well, maybe they need to look into their Bibles more carefully. Take David for example, or Elijah."

Then she noticed that Sam's surprised expression was slowly altering into one of gratitude.

"I knew you were the right person to talk to," he said. "Good job on your Bible knowledge, by the way."

They smiled shyly at each other but then Claire sobered again.

"I really didn't mean to blurt out like that," she said. "I have to admit I don't know what to say. I'm afraid it will all sound useless or insensitive."

"Nothing you say would ever be either of those things," Sam said. "I know you never speak thoughtlessly about anything, even if I don't agree with everything you say. But…" He paused and gripped his jaw. "You do raise another reason why it's hard to tell people. Mental-health issues make people uncomfortable. Either they don't want to acknowledge they exist, or they want to tell the person suffering that they need to 'buck up' or whatever expression they use that means that we should simply be able to talk ourselves into feeling better. Sometimes, they are so uncomfortable they might choose not to be around someone who suffers from mental illness."

Claire sat quietly for a moment. "How can we fix that?" she asked.

"I wish I knew. There are some strides being made in taking away the stigma, but we've got a long way to go."

"Do you think…?" Claire hesitated. "Do you think it could help take some of it away if you *did* talk openly about it, about what you've gone through yourself?"

Sam shook his head. "I'm not ready for that. I know I said I wanted to be more open and, believe me, even telling you was a bigger step than I ever imagined taking. But I still think it's better if I don't give people reason to doubt my shepherding."

Claire nodded slowly. Of course, it was his decision and she knew everything he said about attitudes toward mental illness was true. Still, she would pray about it.

A look of determination settled across Sam's features. "As long as we're talking, there's something else I want you to know, but again, I'm asking you to keep this to yourself."

Claire nodded. "Of course," she said, though her heart pounded with apprehension.

"I've been putting out applications to move to a bigger city, a bigger church."

"You want to leave Living Skies?" Claire was taken aback by the disappointment that ran through her. Wouldn't she be relieved if her nemesis was gone?

Yet she already knew she would never again be able to think of him that way.

"I'm not sure if *want* is the right word," Sam said. "But it is something I feel called to do. Anyway, are you sure you're not hungry? I just saw Michelle go by with a piece of banana-cream pie that looked delicious."

Claire understood it was a signal that he was done sharing for the night and that she needed to respect that, but sometime soon she would let Sam know that she wasn't done with these conversations.

After all, he had chosen to share with her.

"Banana-cream isn't my favorite," she said, "but you go ahead. I'll just finish my coffee here."

Sam also decided to pass on the pie, claiming he didn't want to indulge alone. As they sipped their coffees, they made small talk about various things going on at the church and in town.

Claire noticed that neither of them raised the property beside Love Blooms.

She swallowed the last of her coffee. "I should probably be getting home."

"I've hit you with a lot tonight," Sam said. "I'm sorry about that."

"No, don't apologize." Claire tried to block and interpret the sudden irritation that surged through her. After what Sam had shared with her, she hadn't wanted to fill up the evening chatting about things as if what he'd said was nothing. She didn't want them to feel like they had to avoid the things they disagreed about.

"You have something on your mind," Sam said, not a question.

There were many ways to answer him, but the best Claire

could come up with was "I don't want to treat you any differently."

"Good. I don't want you to."

Michelle chose that moment to reappear with the coffee-pot.

"Not for me, thanks, Michelle," Sam said, and Claire also shook her head, summoning a smile for the hardworking student.

"Okay." Michelle smiled back. "There's no rush, but I'll just bring the bill and you can pay whenever you're ready."

"This one's on me," Sam insisted when Claire reached for her purse.

This one... Did that mean there would be other such outings?

But he's not going to stay.

Outside of Murphy's, Sam turned to Claire and smiled in a way that sent her previous irritation fluttering away.

"Thank you," he said. "For being so wonderful with the youth tonight and for listening." He brushed the sleeve of her cherry-red winter coat with his black-gloved fingers, causing her pulse to rise.

For a moment something hovered between them. Then Sam stepped back. "Talk to you soon," he said, turning to walk to his car.

Claire sat in her own car waiting for the engine to warm up. But even after it was ready to go, she still sat pondering all the things Sam had shared with her.

Wondering why she was disappointed at not being kissed.

It was Friday morning, and a sleety kind of snow dampened the pavement. Sam sat behind his desk in the church office and mustered all the willpower he had to keep a smile, or at least a neutral expression, on his face, while

Dorothy and Patrice Larsen attempted to explain why they thought Claire Casey was the wrong choice to make the flower arrangements for Patrice's wedding.

Since the things he had shared with her—things he had never shared—over coffee after youth group on Wednesday, and how her reaction reinforced that he could trust her, he had an even stronger urge to make things right for her.

"But you sought her out," Sam reminded them, "because you admired her work."

He also reminded himself that he loved these people like family, but that also meant that he knew them well and knew that they could be hard to please, sometimes demanding beyond what was reasonable.

Dorothy lifted her already firm chin, the way she did when she was about to make a point that she expected others to get in line with.

Sam noticed that Patrice imitated the gesture after glancing at her mother out of the corner of her eye, but the gesture lost its impact when she nervously twirled a strand of her long, blond hair around her finger.

"I'm sure when we inform Claire of the decision, she'll be fine with it," Dorothy said.

Something that looked a bit like shame skittered across Patrice's face, but she nodded.

But Sam knew that Claire would be far from fine.

Even though they had avoided talk of the property at coffee the other night, he still knew what the extra money would mean to her.

Why don't I get out of her way, then? She's got enough to deal with.

But something in him persisted that he still had something to prove to himself.

Even though the more entangled he allowed his life to

become with Claire's, the less he was sure exactly what that was.

When Dorothy and Patrice delivered their verdict, Sam knew that Claire would be professional and determined to let the customer be right. But on the inside, she would be trying not to break into pieces.

"I doubt that she'll be fine," he said. He spoke calmly and quietly. He had no wish to upset Dorothy or Patrice or to show any disrespect to them. But he couldn't, in good conscience, let them walk out of his office thinking he supported their decision.

And he definitely wouldn't want Claire to think that he supported it.

Dorothy had been in the process of picking up her purse, but her fingers froze around it. Patrice's face took on an expression of avid interest.

"What do you mean, Sam?" Dorothy appeared genuinely flabbergasted.

There was so much he could say, but he decided to keep it short and to the point, and, ideally, let Dorothy draw her own conclusions.

"It was a big order and Claire runs a small business. An order like that could make a lot of difference to someone like her."

Dorothy tapped one manicured nail on her chin for a few seconds, her brow furrowed. But then, as if aware that doing so could leave a frown line, she quickly relaxed her face.

"Claire does have a gift, no doubt about that," she said, causing hope to course through Sam. A hope that quickly deflated when she said, "I'm sure that she'll find no shortage of business, but, unfortunately, she just wasn't right for us."

"Can't you give her another chance?" Sam persisted. He heard a pleading tone enter his voice, despite his best efforts. "You said yourself that she's gifted, so maybe it's a problem with communication. I'm sure that if you could convey clearly what you had in mind, she'd be able to accommodate you."

"I believe we were quite clear." Dorothy's tone took on a crispness that Sam recognized and knew didn't bode well.

"It's really hard to make decisions about flowers," Patrice added, which he guessed was closer to the truth of why Claire was struggling to please them.

"I'm still willing to help." He was pulling out a last-ditch effort. "You did ask me to be involved."

Dorothy studied him. Something about her scrutiny reminded Sam very much of his mother. Then the corners of her mouth lifted in an assessing kind of smile.

"I think I know what this is all about, Sam," she said. "You care for this girl."

"I care about doing the right thing," Sam said. But he couldn't quite hold Dorothy's gaze.

Dorothy stood. "I'm not going to dispute what I see as an obvious thing," she said. "I'm sorry that things didn't work out better as far as Claire doing the flowers for the wedding, but what happens between the two of you going forward is completely up to you."

Knowing that Dorothy would be determined to have the last word and not knowing what else he could say, anyway, Sam saw no choice other than to stand up as well and escort them to the door.

Patrice waited until her mother was a few steps away and then turned back and quickly whispered, "I liked some of the arrangements, but you know my mother."

Sam's heart ached for her and he thought that it wasn't

likely that Patrice would grow up unless her parents allowed her to. Being under her mother's thumb probably wasn't the best way to enter into a marriage, but that was a whole different matter, and no one was asking for his opinion on that.

As soon as they were gone, he gently closed the door behind them, returned to his desk and sat down, sinking his head into his arms.

As he had told Claire, chronic depression had nothing to do with how he felt about a particular thing at a particular time. But sometimes he knew exactly why he felt a certain way and—sometimes—that could be worse.

Then he lifted his head back up. He had to get to work.

For a few minutes he made a valiant effort to study the notes he had made based on the week's Bible reading passages.

God existed—he believed that—but what His ultimate purpose for Sam was still remained a mystery.

Sam set the notes aside with a sigh. It was no use; he couldn't concentrate until he talked to Claire. But, then again, was it his place to give her a heads-up, or would that be betraying years of connection with the Larsen family, who, despite everything, had always been good to him?

Lord, I could really use some direction here.

His cell phone rang and he answered eagerly, Claire being foremost in his mind.

"Hello? Pastor Sam. This is Shirley Allen speaking."

Sam fought back against his initial disappointment.

He hadn't seen Troy at youth group for a couple of weeks and he'd been concerned. Shame tormented him, telling him he should have reached out. A pastor's weeks had ways of filling up quickly, but that was no excuse.

"It's good to hear from you, Shirley," he said. "How can I help?"

He was so sure that she was going to talk about Troy that it took him a few seconds to register what she was actually saying.

"I'd like to set up a meeting with you to go over some things," she said. "And I wanted to let you know that I plan on Claire Casey being there as well, if she agrees. I know there have been some tensions between the two of you."

Sam didn't know if he should cringe or laugh. He wondered how many people thought that he and Claire truly didn't get along based on their bickering at the town-hall meetings.

Nothing could be further from the truth, at least from his perspective, especially since he trusted Claire enough to have opened up to her the way he did.

If it wasn't about Troy, he wondered what Shirley wanted to talk to both him and Claire about.

He pulled up his online calendar, which Ann kept meticulously updated for him. "I'm free Monday morning— does that work for you? We can meet here at my office."

"That sounds fine," Shirley said. "Thank you, Pastor. How does nine thirty sound?"

Sam entered the date and saved it, sending himself a reminder.

"Sounds good," he said.

"Good," Shirley said with satisfaction. "I was hoping we would have a chance to meet before the next town-council meeting."

What did their meeting have to do with town council?

"I'll give Claire a call back and let her know that we've confirmed a time," Shirley said.

"What about her shop?" Sam asked, half to himself.

"She said she would open earlier and stay open later to make up the lost time, if needed," Shirley explained.

"Thanks again, Sam. I'll let you get back to work. Talk to you soon."

Sam's stomach quivered with unease after they hung up. After knowing of the bad news Dorothy planned to dump on Claire—if she hadn't done so already—he prayed that this wasn't something else that would negatively impact Claire.

Again, he asked himself what he was willing to do if it was. Just the other day, he'd had a phone conversation, referred to as a preliminary interview by the woman who called him, with a church in Edmonton, Alberta, that sounded like it offered a plethora of programs.

Yet, even during the phone call, he'd struggled to put the needs of the church and town he currently served out of his mind.

Do I really want to disappear in the crowd anymore?

He tried to put his focus back on the sermon he'd been working on, but his thoughts now whirled in what felt like a thousand different directions. Because of his illness, concentrating could be difficult at the best of times, but this was something else entirely.

Ann, with her inner radar sharp, as usual, poked her head into his office. "Anything I can get you? Maybe a nice chamomile tea?"

Sam thought of asking for coffee but decided against it because his nerves were already tap-dancing.

"No, thank you," he said.

"Are you sure?" Ann asked. "I saw the look on Dorothy Larsen's face when she left and I figured you might need something calming. I've worked on enough church functions to know how that woman looks when she gets her own way on something—forgive me, Lord, for saying so—which means that someone else didn't get their way."

"I'm worried for Claire Casey," Sam said. It was a relief to say it out loud and he trusted Ann implicitly. "They've decided they don't want her to do the flowers for Patrice's wedding anymore."

A jolt of anger coursed through him, which he paused and breathed through. Getting angry wasn't going to help anything.

Ann eased her way farther in and took a chair without being asked.

"And this concerns you because…?"

"Because? What kind of a question is that?" Sam gaped at his assistant. She was efficient and trustworthy, but she did have an incredible knack for asking questions that made him squirm with discomfort.

I am the pastor, he told himself. *I am a grown man.*

"Because she is a parishioner and I care about what happens to all of the people who attend this church." He sat back, rather pleased with himself.

Ann rolled her eyes skyward as if seeking Heavenly intervention. Then her eyes focused back on him with laser sharpness.

"I'm not buying it." She folded her arms across her chest. "Would you like to try that one more time?"

It took all of Sam's willpower not to break eye contact.

After another beat of silence, Ann said, "You need to be honest about caring for Claire and decide what you're going to do about it. Pray about it, if you have to, though I'm thinking that's a given, with you being a pastor and all."

"I will," Sam said. He would have laughed at the slightly disappointed look on Ann's face, if he'd felt like laughing at all. No doubt, she was looking forward to a good, healthy argument.

Right now he only wanted to be alone with his thoughts

about Claire, about the Larsens' decision and about what Shirley Allen possibly wanted to meet about.

What he did *not* want to think about was how even the astute Ann McFadden couldn't possibly guess that he wasn't sure at all that praying would help him.

Chapter Ten

~

When God closes a door, He always opens a window.

Claire had heard that saying many times. If asked, she
would say she believed it herself. But what it was missing, she now thought, was the ever-so-important detail that
there could be—and probably would be—a very long and
twisting, turning hallway between that closed door and
the open window.

She had done everything she could think of to stay positive about this Saturday morning meeting with Dorothy and
Patrice Larsen and had tried her best to leave it in God's
hands. But she couldn't seem to stop herself from grabbing
it back and running it in circles through her mind like a
hamster on an endless treadmill.

The problem was that no matter how much she told God
that she trusted Him to work things out the way they were
supposed to, the truth was that, inwardly, she was sure that
this opportunity was about to slip through her fingers. She
couldn't, despite her best efforts, find it in herself to trust
that losing this account was the best outcome. Much as she
had tried to stop herself from doing so, she had begun to
count on the extra money coming in and allowed herself
to dream of what she would do with it.

An anxious pair of reflected eyes stared back at Claire

as she brushed her teeth, then smoothed her hair behind her ears, holding one side in place with a bobby pin that sported a snowflake.

"You look pretty, Mommy," Maggie said, leaning in the doorway of the bathroom with an interest that was seasoned with concern, and her compliment had the vibe of someone trying to make someone else feel better.

She's only four years old.

Maggie was precocious, to say the least, but there was no way that Claire was going to let her daughter have anything to worry about.

"Thank you, Magpie." She pasted on a smile and turned from the mirror.

As she did so, she promised herself that she would not go into this with a defeatist attitude. She could still make this work. She *would* still make it work.

She gave Maggie one kiss on each sweet, apple-firm cheek and said, "I'll try to be as quick as I can."

Maggie nodded. "I know you will. Aunt Rachel says I can help her fold laundry."

Claire said, "That sounds good," as she wondered how long it would be before Maggie stopped thinking of chores as a game.

She checked her reflection one last time and was pleased to see herself looking more determined. Her favorite red sweater gave her some confidence.

Dorothy had requested they meet at Murphy's, which returned a bit of Claire's apprehension as she approached the restaurant. Maybe Dorothy had suggested they meet in a public place to prevent a scene.

Taking a deep breath and ordering herself not to assume the worst, Claire entered the restaurant.

"We're over here, Claire." Dorothy waved from a table along the wall, away from the busiest part of the restaurant.

Claire squared her shoulders, said a brief, silent prayer and went to join them. But she hadn't even reached the table when she knew what to expect from this conversation.

Dorothy held her usual expression of unflappable calmness, one that Claire had seen carry her through church events and meetings where disagreements were on the table.

But Patrice had apparently not inherited her mother's mask of "all is well" and it was in her eyes that Claire saw that this meeting was not going to go in her favor.

She slid into the empty seat and Patrice glanced at her with something that looked like an apology, but before Claire could be sure, the bride-to-be shifted her gaze to her mother and stirred her spoon around and around in her tea, although the milk and sugar on their tray were undisturbed.

"Would you like anything?" Dorothy offered. "Tea? Coffee?"

Claire swallowed. Her dry throat could use the comfort of tea, but she wasn't sure if her stomach would agree.

"No, thank you. Water is fine."

"Well, we might as well get right to the point, then," Dorothy said.

Patrice squirmed—actually squirmed—in her chair and for a split second Claire felt sorry for her and considered what she could do to make this meeting as painless as possible.

But then she thought about Maggie and all the opportunities she wanted to be able to give her, and she mentally dug in her heels.

She was not going down without a fight, not only for her daughter's sake, but also for the sake of Love Blooms and everything she'd put into it of herself—her ideas, her creativity, her prayers—to make it the store that it was so far. And she knew it could be so much more.

"I'm sure you won't be entirely surprised at what I'm about to tell you, Claire," Dorothy said. "At least I hope you won't be. You know I haven't been pleased with the flower arrangements you've presented so far, and although I've given you a chance to work with the ideas I've given you, it doesn't seem like we're able to come to an agreement, does it?"

Claire briefly wondered how many times Dorothy could say "I," as if she was the one about to become the bride.

She considered asking Patrice what her thoughts were, since it was her wedding, but it was so obvious that she was used to deferring to her mother that Claire didn't have the heart to put her on the spot that way.

So she kept her focus on Dorothy and, with considerable effort, matched her pleasant tone, as if they were discussing the weather and not the loss of something that Claire had been counting on.

"I'm sure we can work through this, Dorothy." Claire was pleased that her voice held no note of pleading. She didn't sound like she was teetering on the brink of losing everything she had counted on.

"I'm not sure that we can." Dorothy's pleasant tone was edged in steel. It was something Claire had heard before when Dorothy had decided that a matter was settled and done. She had admired that kind of unwavering certainty in the past, but that was before it had been aimed at her.

"I think we have to go in another direction," Dorothy said, letting Claire know that the intent of this meeting wasn't to have a discussion—it was to let her know that the decision had already been made. "I do like you, Claire. I really do. I think it's best that we remain friends and not try to mix business in there. I am willing to acknowledge my mistake in thinking it was a good idea in the first place."

Dorothy lifted her cup and took a sip of her tea with the manner of someone having satisfactorily settled something.

We're not friends.

Claire bit back the reply that wanted to hurl itself out of her mouth. She looked at Patrice, hoping against hope that the young woman would step in. It was her wedding, after all, and Claire honestly thought she'd liked some of the ideas for the arrangements.

But Patrice's tea sat, getting cold, while she twisted her hands in her lap and her cheeks burned a deep pink.

"It would mean everything to me to do these flowers," Claire said. She wouldn't give in. She didn't care anymore if it did sound like she was begging. "I know I'm good at what I do. I'm sorry if it seems like I haven't been listening to your input. I can do a better job at that, I promise."

For the first time, Dorothy looked slightly uncomfortable.

"Let's not do this," she said, her mouth turned slightly downward, as if she had tasted something she didn't like. "I'm afraid my decision isn't going to change."

Claire gathered her dignity and stood.

"All right, then. Thank you for letting me know."

Just as she was about to leave the table, Claire turned and asked, "Does Pastor Sam know?"

"I mentioned my thoughts to him, yes," Dorothy said.

So Sam knew...

Claire hadn't thought it was possible to feel any lower. But she was wrong.

Although Claire usually treasured any extra time she could spend with Maggie on the weekends, on that particular weekend all her energies were focused on trying not to reveal how distraught she was over Dorothy's decision.

After Dorothy Larsen had told her, not leaving room for any argument, that they had decided to go in a different direction for the flowers, Claire had finished up the rest of the day in a state of shock. She knew they weren't seeing eye to eye on some things, but she had always been able to work things out with her customers.

Even now, on Monday morning, she kept tracking the conversation over in her head, thinking that she could have somehow stood up to Dorothy's bulldozing.

It was interesting how her view of Dorothy had changed over the last couple of weeks. She still respected Dorothy. She wasn't the type to lose respect for someone for disagreeing with her. In fact, sometimes she respected them even more.

Like Pastor Sam, for instance...

But what she had not realized was how much Dorothy's calm exterior and quiet voice had housed a steely will that was not to be bent once she had made her mind up about something.

She couldn't explain her disappointment in Sam for not being able to help her, when the truth was that she was the one who had failed to make a good impression.

She was still trying to sort out how she felt about him not giving her a heads-up, although she did understand how torn he must have been.

Or maybe he wasn't torn at all. His friendship with the Larsens had existed much longer than his friendship with her—if that was what she could even call what they had between them.

Sometimes she wasn't sure if they were even friends, yet other times, when she remembered a certain look in his eyes or had memorized his voice saying she was beautiful, she thought they could be so much more.

But Sam had made it clear that he planned to leave at the first opportunity. The truth of this jabbed at Claire like a sharp needle.

But now she had to put all of those thoughts on hold as she got ready and pondered what Shirley Allen had on her mind that she needed to talk to both her and Sam about.

It was a beautiful winter morning, so Claire left her car at home and walked to the church. She had paid a bit extra for boots with good treads on them, but it was well worth it to give her more security on the potential icy patches.

She had developed the habit whenever she walked, or did any exercise routine, of thanking God for the body He had given her; that it was strong and healthy, and that she could walk and take in the world He had created.

As she walked that morning, Claire took in the sights and sounds that told her that Living Skies was into the Christmas season. Storefronts were decorated, colored lights were wrapped around streetlamps, and soon the lighting of the tree at Town Hall would take place and the life-size Nativity scene would be displayed outside Good Shepherd Church.

It gave her a cheery but unmistakable nudge that she could be doing a lot more at home to bask in the season, not only for Maggie's sake, but also for her own.

If there was ever a time she needed to be fully aware of God's gifts, it was now.

With her thoughts leaping between prayer and speculation on the upcoming meeting, Claire arrived at the church more quickly than she'd wanted to.

She paused on the steps to brush off her pants, stomp snow off her boots and to take a few deep, prayerful breaths before going in.

Ann McFadden was in the lobby watering the plants.

"Hi, Ann," Claire greeted her.

"Good morning, Claire," Ann said with a smile. "The others are already in the fellowship room."

Claire had enjoyed many memorable, faith-enriching gatherings in that room. But now, as she headed toward it, wondering what was in store for the morning, it didn't seem nearly as welcoming.

The first person her eyes fell on when she entered the room was Sam, almost like they were trained to gravitate toward him. He wore blue jeans and a plaid flannel shirt in shades of light and darker greens. The color looked great on him.

He really is handsome.

"Hi, Claire. Glad you could make it."

It wasn't Sam who'd given the greeting. His eyes clung to hers, too.

Claire tore her gaze away.

Had anyone noticed?

"Hi, Shirley." She turned to greet her friend, whose expression showed that she was anxious to forgo the formalities and get the meeting underway.

Her obvious anxiousness made Claire's tap-dancing nerves beat double time, but at least Shirley hadn't seemed to notice, or care, how she and Sam looked at one another.

"We're just waiting for..." Sam began, and Claire was even more puzzled. Whom else were they waiting for?

She was aware of her eyebrows arching in surprise when Grace Bishop entered with Gloria clinging to her hand.

Grace caught her eye and nodded. Her eyes spelled out determination.

"Grace and I ran into each other at Graham's yesterday," Shirley explained, referring to the town's grocery store. "We got to talking, and I just found myself wanting to share what we were meeting about today, and she wanted to come and share her thoughts as well."

A glimmer of hope sparked in Claire. She still didn't know what this meeting was about, but both Shirley and Grace had expressed support of her Love Blooms' expansion at the town meetings, and knowing they were on her side about that lessened the anxiety she felt over this meeting.

"The staff is having a professional development day at Gloria's school," Grace added. "So it worked out great that she was able to come with me. This concerns her, too, and I think she's old enough to be part of the discussion."

Claire knew that Grace was determined not to shelter Gloria and wanted to help her live up to her full potential, but hearing that this morning's meeting also concerned Gloria made her stomach flip-flop back into the nervousness.

Sam's professional pastor face wore a mask of neutrality, but she knew he must have as many questions as she did. Ever since he had confided in her about his depression, Claire found herself increasingly aware of the inner strength and gritty faith it must take him to present that face to the world each day.

A man like that was someone she would trust in her life.

"Hi, everybody." Gloria grinned and waved. She was her usual friendly self and didn't appear to be showing any emotional scars from the teasing Claire had witnessed in her store.

Yet, Claire knew from experience, something was there beneath the surface. Once the seeds of bullying had been planted, they didn't always stay buried but could spring up into a mess of harmful weeds.

"Let's get this meeting started, so we can hear what you have on your mind, Shirley." Sam's suggestion echoed Claire's thoughts.

Since there weren't many of them, they chose one of the smaller round tables to sit at. Sam opened with a word of prayer. Claire sat to his right. She breathed in his clean, comforting scent and her hand itched to reach out to seek, and to offer, reassurance.

"Amen," she said, echoing the others, and her hands gripped her purse instead.

"Shirley, the floor is yours," Sam said.

"Thank you, Pastor." Shirley took a deep breath. "Well, I guess the first thing I'll do is start with something I need to tell you..." She gestured at him. "And you," she continued, expanding the gesture to include Claire.

Claire became aware that she was holding her breath and made herself let it out. The soft, whooshing sound drew Sam's eyes to hers again. His smile was sympathetic.

Grace had taken a book off the shelf and she and Gloria were pointing at pictures in it, murmuring in soft undertones.

"Okay, here's the thing." Shirley took another deep breath before exhaling. "I've made my own offer on the property by your flower shop, Claire. There's going to be discussion at the next town-council meeting, but I've been told that will just be a formality." She looked apologetic but determined. "I gave considerable thought to some of the incidents lately that have impacted my son Troy, and Gloria here," Shirley said.

Gloria looked up at the sound of her name and smiled a little before returning to the book.

"I still respect and admire the work you do, Claire," Shirley continued, "and that's one of the reasons I wanted to personally tell you of this decision. I've come to believe that what Sam wants to do will benefit the greatest number of people. I do understand that the idea has our newcomers at the core of that, and I agree with all that can mean. But literal newcomers are not the only ones being left out, not finding their place, and I can't live with that." Shirley's eyes were sad and thoughtful.

"I don't know exactly how we should use the property. I do know that we don't need another church. But I'm sorry, Claire. Much as I want to support your dream of expanding your flower shop, I just can't believe that's enough anymore."

Breath whooshed out of Claire, leaving her deflated like a punctured balloon.

She wanted both to look at Sam and to refuse to look at him.

If she saw any hint, any hint at all from him that he had known this would happen, she didn't know if she would be able to stop herself from leaving the room.

But when her eyes found his face, almost of their own accord, she could tell that he was as taken aback as she was.

The troubled cloud in his eyes seemed to say that he wasn't sure he was happy to get what he'd wanted if it meant hurting her in the process.

Or maybe she was only seeing what she wanted to see.

Sometimes Sam got distracted by Claire Casey's eyes and it was a challenge to pay attention to anything else.

What he saw in them now was the shock of betrayal… and the assurance she sought that he hadn't been in on it.

He tried his best to silently convey that he'd had no idea this was coming.

First the Larsens. Now this.

Sam had the sure and sudden conviction that he would

no longer be able to be happy with anything that was going
to make Claire Casey unhappy.

And with that came the equally strong conviction, as
if God had whispered the answer directly in his ear, that
leaving Good Shepherd and Living Skies for a different
city and church was not the right thing to do.

"You're both awfully quiet," Shirley said. Her eyes darted
between them and she lightly tapped the pen she was holding on the table. "I didn't mean to upset you. I do believe
it's the best decision."

Ann, bless her, made an appearance then, wheeling a
cart with a coffee carafe, hot water for tea, cups and sau-
cers and milk and sugar.

"Thanks, Ann," Sam said, knowing, as his intuitive assistant probably did as well, that the small ritual of fixing
their coffee or tea would help them all take a breath and
prepare for what was ahead.

Ann had also remembered to include a glass of apple
juice, which was Gloria's favorite. Gloria took a hearty sip
and her eyes sparkled with pleasure.

As Sam took a sip of his own coffee, the thought struck
him that, although there were guaranteed to be finer blends
served in fancier places, nothing tasted like the coffee he
shared within these walls with people he cared about.

He purposely caught Claire's eye and raised his cup,
hoping the gesture said, *You're not alone.*

Her face was unreadable, but, after a pause, she raised
her cup in return.

Braced by the familiar camaraderie of having coffee,
they returned to the small table and Sam said, "I know I
opened with prayer, but I think another one could help us
gather our thoughts for an open and respectful discussion."

Sitting beside him, Claire shifted ever so slightly, not in

an impatient way but as if she was settling into the moment, choosing to trust fully in the potential of prayer.

The movement and her flowery scent calmed him in a way he didn't quite understand.

If only I could have her always by my side…

"Our Heavenly Father," Sam prayed, "we know that You are with us. We ask that Your Holy Spirit keep our minds and hearts open in this conversation, and may our words to one another be seasoned with love. In Jesus's name we ask this, amen."

The others echoed, "Amen."

Shirley was the type to get right down to business, so she immediately said, "I think it would be good to hear from Grace now."

Grace nodded. "Yes, thanks, Shirley. I have some things I need to share that I already know you'll be able to relate to, and I hope, Claire, that you'll understand my reasons for also supporting Sam."

Sam restrained himself from turning in Claire's direction. He wanted to give Grace the courtesy of listening fully to what she had to say, even while he was thinking of what he could say or do so that Claire's dream didn't have to die.

He thought again about his decision to let go of his own dream of pastoring a larger church, but still his heart told him it was the right decision.

"As you know," Grace continued, "Gloria attends an intensive support school in Regina. It allows her to be part of mainstream schooling as much as possible while still getting the additional attention and help she needs. I always want Gloria to believe she can accomplish whatever she sets her mind to. I'm sure we all want everyone to feel that way."

Sam knew that Claire certainly wanted Maggie to grow

up with that kind of confidence. He glanced in her direction, trying to gauge her reaction.

"I've always respected your approach to things, Grace," Claire said.

The words were the right things to say, but the sadness that radiated off her crawled into him like it was his own. Not part of the depression he perpetually carried with him, but something sharp and separate.

He somehow knew then that it wasn't just about the news Claire was getting today.

Dorothy has talked to her.

And he knew she must feel like things were crumbling around her.

"I appreciate that," Grace said. She looked at Sam. "You've always wanted a place where newcomers felt welcome. Like Shirley said, I think in a sense we can feel like outsiders when we are ostracized or made fun of. We all need a safe space. This doesn't exempt the support we still want to give them, but our hope is that it will help even more to weave them into the larger fabric, while still achieving what's important to us."

Shirley turned her attention to Claire again.

"I can only imagine what you must be feeling right now, Claire. Grace and I have always been supportive of your running your own business, and please trust me when I say that we still plan to be supportive of that in as many ways as we can be."

Grace nodded intently in agreement.

"This is not meant in any way to betray you, though I'm not questioning it could feel that way. I just know this is what we need to do."

"I do still value both of your friendships," Claire said.

"I just wish you could have given me some idea of what was coming, but it is what it is."

Sam rubbed his hand down his face.

"I still hope we can come up with something that helps Claire, too," he said, turning Claire's startled eyes in his direction.

They stared at each other until Grace gently cleared her throat and the pink that swooshed into Claire's cheeks told Sam that the room had momentarily disappeared for her as well.

He gathered himself.

"We have our Wednesday-night programs, and in previous church-board meetings, we've agreed that the room is outgrowing itself, right?"

Shirley nodded and Grace said, "Yes."

He looked at Claire. "Can I tell them about when you came to talk to youth group?"

She shifted in her chair and furrowed her brow. "I guess, if you want to."

Sam spent the next few minutes openly expressing his admiration for Claire's connection with the youth that night.

When he finished, even Gloria had stopped her coloring and was watching him, and Shirley wore an expression that said that maybe she was aware of something that he—or Claire—wasn't.

"We all agree that Claire is a wonderful person," she said, "but what does that have to do with our future plans?"

"Because it made me realize that once-a-week drop-in classes based on whatever subjects and volunteers we have available aren't enough. We need consistent education, we need mentors, not only for the newcomers, but also for anyone who may be struggling to find their place."

Sam could feel his pulse quickening as the ideas came

like fireworks into his brain. "We've already agreed that we need more space, but I think what we need to agree on is that we need resources, we need an itinerary of everything we can offer, we need advertising and, most of all, we need people like Claire."

"I have a business already," Claire said, her eyes flashing. "I have a daughter."

"I know," Sam said almost desperately, "I know. I am trying to figure out a way that this can all work. That is—" he paused and reminded himself again that this wasn't all about Claire, although it was her heart he realized he most wanted to protect "—if Shirley and Grace can agree with me that it's worth the effort to come up with some kind of compromise."

"I agree," Shirley said thoughtfully. "You know we've always supported you. Claire and I don't want to do anything that makes your life difficult. But I'm trying to keep the bigger picture in mind here. I'm still open to ideas, though."

Grace glanced at her watch. "I need to get Gloria to her dance class and it seems like some things have been raised that I don't think we'll settle this morning. I agree with Shirley, though. I'm open to more discussion."

"I'll close with prayer," Sam said.

After he finished, they all stood and began to gather their belongings.

"Claire," Sam said hurriedly in an undertone, "I'd like to continue this discussion with you…please."

"I have to open Love Blooms," Claire said with a slightly defeated tone to her voice.

"Could I meet you after work, then?" Sam persisted. "It's important to me that we figure this out."

"Well, ultimately it's not our decision anymore," she reminded him, as the other two women waved their goodbyes.

"But they did say they would listen."

Finally, Claire nodded slowly. "I guess it couldn't hurt."

Sam grasped her hands and gave them a little squeeze. "Thank you," he said, "Thank you."

He turned before he gave in to the urge to draw her into a hug, before he could tell her that making her happy was starting to matter to him more than anything else.

Chapter Eleven

A s promised, Sam was waiting outside of her flower shop when Claire closed up for the day.

The sight of him waiting for her was something she could get used to. It was just too bad that she knew he wanted to leave Living Skies.

There was no mistaking it for a summer evening, but the weather remained warm in comparison to many Saskatchewan Decembers. Sam wore black pants, chunky men's work boots and a down-filled black vest over a bulky gray sweater. His hands were in his pockets and his head was down, so she couldn't read his expression.

Claire knew that some people suffered during the shorter days and she thought she must remember to ask Sam how that impacted him.

To her, there had always been a dark beauty in winter, not only when Christmas was approaching, but also throughout the season. She always saw the Creator in her flowers, but she also saw Him in the stars that lit the blue-black sky and even in the silent darkness of the sky itself.

She wondered why Sam had insisted that her goals and wishes be considered, especially when he was about to get what he wanted.

The answer that came to mind, she didn't dare hope was the correct one.

Some people were meant for relationships, but she was not. The fact that when they were arranging this meeting, Sam had told her that he'd decided not to seek other employment after all, didn't change her belief about that. It was too ingrained in her by how she'd been treated in the past.

Resisting the urge to check her lipstick before exiting, Claire stepped outside and said, "I hope I didn't keep you waiting long."

"It's a beautiful night."

They stood and looked at each other for a moment and Claire realized that she hadn't entirely thought this through.

"So…what now?" Sam asked.

"Would you like to come and have supper with us?" The words tumbled out of her mouth in a hurry to beat all the reasons she could give herself for not asking.

The soft surprise and pleasure in Sam's eyes assured her it was the right thing to do.

When they arrived at her place, Claire opened the door and called out, "Hello, I've brought some company home with me."

She purposely hadn't given herself time to think through how her home would look through Sam's eyes—she often described it as clean but lived-in—and she hoped that Sam wouldn't mind all the signs that a busy, inquisitive four-year-old lived there.

Somehow, she knew he wouldn't. Sam could come across as aloof, for reasons she understood better now, but he was never out to find flaws in people.

Instead of the comfortable mess of toys, books and a collage of boots at the front door, however, they stepped into a house that gleamed and had the lemony smell of a recent cleaning.

Maggie ran to greet them and bounced with eagerness.

Claire noticed that she wore her favorite winter dress, a dark green knit with long sleeves and a skirt that flared out. Her hair was brushed neatly and held into place with a headband of snowflakes.

Claire was torn between being pleased at the utter cuteness of her daughter and the company-ready house, and wondering exactly what was going on. She couldn't help noticing that her daughter seemed to find it perfectly acceptable that Sam was with her.

You have to love children's ability to go with the flow, she mused.

"Don't you look pretty?" Claire gave Maggie a brief hug. "Where's Aunt Rachel?"

"We are *ce-le-brating*," Maggie said, enunciating the last word carefully.

"I'm here." Rachel hurried out of the kitchen, causing the scent of their favorite winter stew, with its savory meat, earthy mushrooms and root vegetables, to come wafting into the room.

Unlike Maggie, her face registered surprise, but that was quickly replaced by a welcoming smile, although Claire had no doubt her sister would take the first opportunity she could to pepper her with questions.

"It looks like I'm interrupting something," Sam said. His tone indicated that he was ready to do whatever was polite, but Claire caught wistfulness in his eyes she hadn't seen before and she knew she couldn't ask him to leave, even if she had wanted to.

"Maggie said it's a celebration?" she asked Rachel, while her eyes signaled "we'll talk about my guest later." "Well, the more the merrier, right? Actually —" she decided to offer a brief explanation "—Sam and I have some business things to talk about after supper.

"So—" her eyes went back and forth between Maggie and Rachel "—what are we celebrating?"

Rachel paused for dramatic effect. "I got the job at the art gallery!"

"Oh, Rach, that's wonderful." Claire hugged her sister. "You're so talented and you truly deserve it."

She meant every word, but she still couldn't stop her mind from doing recalculations about what this would mean to her schedule, as she considered different full-time child-care arrangements, and how now it might make it even harder to become part of whatever Shirley and Grace had planned for the property beside her.

Don't be selfish.

She knew that it was a good thing for Rachel to have a job— it was what she wanted and encouraged. But why did it seem like even good news had to come with something tough clinging to it?

"Congratulations, Rachel," Sam said in his quiet, sincere way. "I'll look forward to hearing more about it while we eat."

"The kitchen is that way," Rachel said and pointed, "if you want to wash up first. Maggie can show you where to sit."

Maggie, happy with her role as tour guide, grabbed his hand and hopped beside him as she led him to the kitchen.

Claire heard her daughter as she asked him, "Did you know that turnips are rich in iron and calcium?" and she shook her head, smiling.

"I'm sorry I won't be able to be as much help with Maggie," Rachel said to her when they were alone.

"It will work out," Claire said, a bit ashamed of her earlier thoughts. "This is a good thing."

"So…the pastor…"

"I told you we have some things to talk about." Claire flushed lightly. Then the flush deepened at her sister's grin.

"We had a meeting at the church this morning with Shirley Allen and Grace Bishop about the property," she quickly explained. "I'm not sure how much I can say right now, but, trust me, this is business."

"Oh, really?" Rachel raised a curious eyebrow. "Well, I'll be interested to hear more details about that when you can share them. But there's no way that man in our kitchen is here just on business. Can't you see how he looks at you?"

Claire found that she didn't want to immediately push away the idea, but she just replied, "Let's go and eat. It smells delicious."

Indeed, the stew was delicious and conversation flowed as Rachel provided the details she had so far about her new job, while Maggie chirped in with her precocious opinions.

Sam sat across from Claire and every so often their eyes would meet, and for the first time in as long as she could remember, her imagination wandered to what it would be like to have a man be part of her and Maggie's lives.

No, not just any man, but Sam Meyer, with his kindness and his caring attentiveness.

But, no, as she'd told Rachel, this was about making different kinds of decisions.

After supper, Claire left Sam chatting with Rachel, wanting, as always, to be the one taking Maggie through her bedtime routine.

Following bedtime prayer, Maggie gazed up with her wide eyes and said, "I really like Pastor Sam, Mommy. He should come over more often."

Okay, is my whole family in on this idea?

"He is a nice man," she agreed, even while thinking that

he was so much more than nice. He was someone she could imagine a life with…if she imagined that sort of thing.

She kissed Maggie on the forehead and once on each cheek. "Sweet dreams."

When she returned to the kitchen, Sam was stacking dishes back into the cupboard while Rachel gave directions, as she rinsed and draped the dishcloth over the faucet.

The sight of it clenched Claire's heart into longing.

"I should let you two talk," Rachel said breezily. "See you later."

She retreated to her room and Claire said, "Let's go sit in the living room."

She could sense Sam taking in the room.

"This is very you," he said. "Warm, bright. I like it."

"Thank you."

Claire could almost sense a shift in the air between them.

"Please, sit anywhere you want," she said hurriedly as she gestured around.

"I really enjoyed supper and the company," Sam said. He put a slight emphasis on the word *enjoyed* and Claire understood what he was telling her. She knew his depression would never go away, but he was letting her know that she had brought some light into his day.

He had trusted her with something deep and true about himself. Maybe it was time she trusted him.

She sat on the end of the couch, near the chair Sam had chosen.

"Haven't you ever wondered about Maggie's father?" she asked.

Sam blinked, clearly showing this wasn't what he'd been expecting to talk about.

"I've been curious on occasion," Sam replied, recovering from his surprise. "But mostly because I'd like to meet the man and ask him what's wrong with him. Who would give up someone like you, not to mention a sweet girl like Maggie?"

Claire swallowed. The words were like a balm, but she couldn't let herself count on them or need them. That was what she wanted Sam to understand.

"He never met Maggie and he didn't want anything to do with the pregnancy," she said, "and he hardly knew me. I know that must sound really bad."

Sam shook his head, his expression holding nothing but compassion.

"He was in town on a construction project," Claire continued. "He gave me a lot of attention, said all of the right things. I wasn't used to that kind of attention. We've talked about what school was like for me. I fell for it hard and fast. Of course, as soon as he got what he wanted, he didn't find me nearly as appealing."

"That's on him, Claire, not you," Sam said gently.

Does he know he's stroking my hand?

She eased hers back, not because she didn't like the reassuring gesture but because she didn't want to like it too much.

"Anyway, since then I haven't let myself need that kind of attention. I don't really trust it, if I'm being honest, and I guess it's all kind of snowballed, so I don't really like accepting help from anyone, especially a man," Claire admitted. Sam might as well know the whole truth.

"Was it difficult for you to make the decision to keep Maggie?" Sam asked. "I hope that people were kind to you." He frowned, as though worried they hadn't been.

"It was a shock to some people, yes," Claire said, "and I'm sure they had their opinions, but they have their own road to walk with God. I can only walk mine. I knew I had made a mistake, but I also knew I could repent of it and be forgiven. I don't say that lightly or take it for granted, not at all. As far as keeping Maggie, it never felt like I had a choice. Giving her up would have been like tearing me into pieces."

Sam nodded.

"I'm always able to be strong for Maggie," Claire added, "but lately there are things that have rocked my self-confidence."

"I knew this whole thing with Patrice's wedding flowers was difficult for you," Sam said slowly. "But I didn't fully understand how it must have felt for you not to be able to fix things yourself. Thank you for telling me."

Claire slumped her shoulders. "They're not fixed, anyway," she sighed. She briefly reiterated her Saturday meeting with Dorothy and Patrice.

Sam's eyes flashed anger on her behalf. "I have half a mind to tell them…"

He broke off in midsentence as Claire shook her head.

"Okay, I get that you don't want to need me," Sam said after a moment. "But…what if we needed each other?" He hurried on before she could respond too quickly. "I could use a friend, you already know more about me than most people do and I care about you. I really do."

Claire studied her hands folded in her lap so they wouldn't tremble. "I…care about you, too, and I guess I could use a good friend. I don't really open up to many people, either, and I do trust you."

Her heart lifted and floated before reality punctured it again. "But I can't get too attached to you, Sam, even if you are staying like you said. I just don't have it in me."

But, with him sitting there, she longed more than anything to trust enough in relationships to feel differently.

In the meantime, she was sure that she wanted to keep talking to this man, brainstorming ideas for the property, yes, but also telling him stories about her childhood, hearing more about his life, discussing the merits of counseling for depression and even laughing about their mutual love for British comedy.

She didn't want the warm cloak of comfort that enveloped her to disappear, even if it meant that they didn't talk about uses for the property as much as they should have.

Somehow, sharing the evening with Sam made it easier to believe that there would be a solution.

He wasn't her nemesis anymore. He was someone who cared about her future.

At the end of the evening, it felt right and natural for Sam's arms to go around her. She allowed herself to relax into them. Then she felt the lightest of strokes on her hair and a soft kiss at the side of her face.

She stepped back, not angry but taken aback.

"I'm sorry," Sam said immediately. "I just… I think the world of you, Claire."

"It's okay. I just didn't… I didn't know it was like that."

Sam was quiet for a few seconds. "I don't think I did, either."

Claire emboldened herself then. She leaned back in and kissed the side of his face then, softly, kissed his surprised and pleased mouth.

After Sam left, Claire went through her getting-ready-for-bed routine with an alertness to possibilities she hadn't felt for a long time.

She lay awake a long time that night thinking about instigating the kiss. It wasn't at all like her, at least not when it came to any kind of relationship. Though, when she thought about it, she didn't have any problems being spontaneous with other parts of her life.

Sam had said he no longer wanted to leave.

Was it finally time for her to take a chance with her heart?

* * *

"I got the coffee supplies, Pastor." Ann's head popped into Sam's office the following morning.

"Oh, good," he said distractedly. He was trying to write a teaching for the children on sharing. So far he had written *Sharing is*.

Brilliant.

There was no denying that his focus wasn't on teaching. No, instead he was replaying the kiss he'd shared with Claire—the warmth of her lips—on a giddy repeating reel through his mind.

"Would you like a cup?" Ann asked as she lingered.

"A cup?"

"Of coffee," Ann said with notable patience. "The stuff I just went to get supplies for."

"Ah, right. No, thanks."

Ann gave him a look before going to make herself a cup.

She returned and, holding her mug, which boasted that she was a proud grandmother, looked out the window at the snow falling outside.

"More snow," she remarked. She turned back to Sam. "You know, I love Christmas and I try to find something to appreciate about all the seasons, but if this keeps up, I might have to make a trip to visit my cousin in Regina. They have a lovely city greenhouse there and her church has an indoor community garden, which really gives me a lift at this time of year. We could use one here."

Sam set down his pen and every nerve in his body went on high alert.

Community garden. Of course. It's so obvious I can't believe we didn't think of it.

"Ann," he said as he stood up, unable to contain the energy that flooded through him. "You're a genius."

"So some have claimed," Ann said in her unflappable way. "What have I managed to do now?"

"You have just given me an idea that I think we can make work for everyone involved."

"Great. Let me know how it all turns out." She helped herself to a gingersnap from the cookie tin on Sam's desk and returned to her own station.

Thoughts and plans raced through Sam's mind.

Could this be the answer, Lord?

If Shirley and the town council agreed to a community garden, that would be something that Claire could be a part of and make a huge contribution to without having to be away from her shop. She could be their major supplier, which would increase her bottom line, and maybe, as her time allowed, she could teach and mentor others in the craft of flower arranging and other things.

Not to mention, it would be something that others could genuinely be part of. Whether it was a newcomer to the town or a longtime resident, young or old, he could visualize it with benches, places to read and visit, places to plant and tend gardens. It could be a way for people to bond, to feel soothed and invigorated by the power of God's creations around them.

He picked up the phone and called Claire.

"Hello?" she answered.

"Hi, Claire. Did I catch you at a busy time?"

"No, not really. How are you?"

Sam could hear the new shy awareness of him in her voice and he smiled.

"I'm good. I was hoping we could meet if you're able to take a lunch break today. I have something I want to talk over with you.

"It's a good thing," he added, hearing her hesitation.

"Okay," Claire said. "I can make time to meet, but I'll need to stay around the shop."

"I'll come there," Sam said. "Is around twelve thirty okay?"

"Yes, that should be fine... Sam?"

"Yes?"

"I've been thinking about you."

Sam said, "Same here... About you, I mean." He couldn't remember a time when happiness wasn't an elusive wisp of something slipping through his fingers.

It wasn't that he thought his depression had or would magically disappear. But with Claire's support, he could at least believe he could manage it.

He could believe that maybe he wasn't meant to be alone after all.

"How about I pick up some sandwiches for us from Murphy's?" he suggested. "Do you have any favorites? Any allergies?"

"No to the latter, and surprise me," Claire said.

At lunchtime, Sam arrived at Love Blooms holding a bag that held two sandwiches, an assortment of green and purple grapes and two of the pastry chef's renowned dark-chocolate-chip cookies.

"Thank you," Claire said, accepting the wrapped sandwich from him. "It's a treat to have someone pick up lunch for me. We can sit here." She indicated the counter where she had instructed him to sit when he first came into the shop.

It seemed a lifetime ago.

"You said to surprise you," Sam said as they sat and Claire began to unwrap her sandwich. "I got us both my favorite. I hope you approve."

He eagerly watched her sample the Black Forest ham, Swiss cheese, sprouts and lightly salted tomatoes on the restaurant's famous homemade grainy bread.

She chewed and swallowed. "Oh, that is so good."

"It's nothing fancy," Sam said, pleased at her enjoyment. "But I find that good-quality simple ingredients make the best meals."

"I completely agree."

Sam found himself imagining them preparing and appreciating meals together. That he was able to have this thought gave him such hope, as his illness could play cruel games with his appetite.

They didn't make much conversation as they indulged in the delicious food that had been provided, but Sam knew that Claire would only have so much time to spare in her day and he was anxious to share his thoughts with her before the next customer came in.

He reiterated what Ann had said and his immediate reaction, the deep certainty, that this was the answer they'd been looking for.

Claire furrowed her brow thoughtfully. Sam could see a light of cautious hope in her eyes but suspected she was reining herself in from prematurely letting that hope take flight.

He didn't want to lift her expectations only to see them take a fall, but he had such a feeling in his heart about this one, almost as if God was whispering in his ear, telling him that it was the right thing to do, that he couldn't help urging her to see the potential.

"Everyone would come to you, Claire. They know and trust you and they know your work."

There was a pause, ever so lightly sprinkled with tension, and Sam hurried past one particular customer who neither of them would mention.

"You could sell people what they needed," he continued. "You could mentor, you could teach classes on flower arranging, and I'm sure you could set your own schedule, and with it being a community endeavor, Maggie could be with you, or playing with the other kids."

"It does sound wonderful, Sam," Claire said. "But we still have to talk to Shirley and, if she agrees, it still has to pass through council. But I do have to admit—" a mischievous grin lit up her face "—I am looking forward to seeing the looks on their faces."

"Shirley's and Grace's?" Sam asked, after he had swallowed the last morsel of chocolate decadence.

"No, town council's faces when they hear that we're actually on the same side about something."

Sam laughed, but he understood the significance of his own words when he said, "I'll be right by your side, Claire. You can count on me."

Watching the expression in her eyes change from wariness to trust was everything he needed to tell him that he had made the right decision to stay.

There was only going to be one more town-council meeting before Christmas, so Sam knew they would have to move quickly to get the others on board and to get the item added to the agenda.

When they met with Shirley and Grace the next evening, both of them quickly warmed to the idea.

"I think it would be a wonderful use of the property," Shirley said. "I can visualize it being a welcoming, nurturing space, which is just what we wanted."

"I agree," Grace added, "and it's something that can be developed and expanded over time."

"If you two—" Shirley gestured to Sam and Claire "—want to take the lead on the presentation to council, I'd be good with that. Your passion for the project is clear and I'm sure that will come across. I'm also glad," she added, "that this could benefit you, Claire."

"I'm glad, too," Sam said, and the look he saw exchanged between Shirley and Grace, along with Claire's blush, told him that he had spoken more fervently than he'd intended.

But he didn't mind. No, he didn't mind at all.

In the days leading up to the meeting, they spent most of their planning time at Claire's condo, because with Maggie that was what was easiest for her. And Sam's depression, though it would never just go away, seemed to him like it was softened at the edges by a sense of home so strong that it overshadowed the home he'd grown up in.

One evening, when Claire returned from tucking Maggie in, Sam, who was sitting at the kitchen table, remarked, "You know, I'm a decent story reader, too. I'm especially good with animal voices."

"I know." Claire rolled her eyes teasingly at him. "I've heard you tell the story of Noah's Ark."

She walked past him to the cupboard. "Tea?" she asked, looking over her shoulder.

"No, thanks. Claire, come sit down with me, please."

"I know we need to get back to work," she said. "Let me just make myself a quick cup."

"I'm not worried about the presentation," Sam said. "I thought that while Rachel was out we could just enjoy a visit."

"Okay…" She quickly made her cup of tea and joined him at the table.

"So talk," she said in her Claire-like way, as her aqua eyes gazed at him.

"I wanted you to know," Sam said, "that I'm enjoying this."

"This?" she asked tentatively.

"Planning with you," Sam said, "being on the same side, getting to know what an amazing person you are… Being with you."

Claire flushed and lowered her eyes. She added a half teaspoonful of sugar to her tea and stirred it with a slightly trembling hand.

"Claire?"

"Yes?"

"Those fairy-tale weddings you pretend about… Did you ever think any of them might be yours?"

She shook her head, her voice almost a whisper when it came out. "I don't believe that for myself, no."

"That's a shame," Sam said. Even if it couldn't be him offering it to her, he wanted that for her. She deserved that and so much more, if she could only realize it.

He got up from his chair and walked around to sit in the one beside her. She smelled of daffodils, a gentle rain and good, clean earth.

He slid his chair over until their knees touched under the table. She didn't pull away.

"Claire," Sam began, brushing his fingertips up and down her arm. "Please don't give up on that dream for yourself. You are so very beautiful and I don't just mean the way that you look. You deserve to be happy in every possible way."

Claire put her warm hand over his and turned to fully face him.

"Sometimes when I'm with you," she said, tears shining in her eyes, "I can almost believe that's true."

On the last night before the meeting, they sat in at Claire's kitchen table, drinking peppermint tea and finalizing the finer points of the presentation.

"I don't know why I'm so nervous," Claire said, her fingertips lightly tapping the side of her teacup.

"I'll be right there to support you," Sam assured her.

"I appreciate that but, if I'm being completely honest, it's not helping my nerves right now. How are you doing?"

"I'll tell you what…" Sam reached out and took Claire's hand, gently curling his fingers around it. "We'll lean on each other."

He wondered if it would be too soon to say that he didn't mean just for the presentation, but that he saw their bond only growing stronger in the days ahead, especially after the vulnerable moment they had shared the other evening at her place.

He was starting to imagine a real future for them.

Claire closed her fingers around his.

"I like the sound of that," she said.

The morning of the council meeting dawned, and the second Sam opened his eyes, he knew.

Something was wrong. Something was very wrong.

The darkness slammed into his mind like a cruelly laughing beast, mocking him for daring to believe he could overcome it.

A small, fighting part of him knew he *had* to overcome. Today was the town-council meeting and Claire was counting on him. He had promised her he would be there and he knew full well what a broken promise would do to her fragile trust, when she already found it difficult to count on others.

He knew all of this.

But the beast was back with a vengeance, knocking him down into the black, swirling cesspool of his mind, telling him that he couldn't do it, he wasn't worthy and that the days he believed differently were all a lie.

Chapter Twelve

Claire wasn't at all surprised to find herself with a stomach full of jitters on the morning of the town-council meeting. But they were a good kind of jitters, the kind filled with hope, like when she'd opened the doors of Love Blooms for the first time, or when Maggie's infant eyes first looked into hers to remind her of what an incredible gift she'd been given to care for.

The kind she felt when Sam promised to be by her side.

Rachel had gone out early to meet some of her future coworkers for breakfast, a tradition the gallery owner insisted upon because, as she said, some socializing outside of work made them a better bonded team.

Already, things were changing. Soon Rachel would be full-force into her new job, making new acquaintances, and eventually she might even want to get her own place.

All of these were good things. It would take some adjustment, but it was what Claire wanted for her sister.

She inspected her reflection one last time and was reasonably satisfied with how she looked in her royal blue sweater and blue-and-green-plaid tartan skirt with royal blue stockings.

"How's that cereal coming along, Magpie?" she asked

her daughter, as she walked into the kitchen fastening in some dangly earrings that complemented her outfit.

"It's not good to rush when you're eating," Maggie informed her. "You could end up with a tummy ache."

"Very true. I'm not trying to rush you, but I did explain that I have a meeting this morning and I'm sure that Gloria is excited to see you."

Maggie was going to spend the morning with Grace's husband, John, and Gloria. His work as a photojournalist and newspaper editor often allowed him to stay home.

After Christmas, Claire would need to apply for a permanent place for Maggie at the preschool.

"She is excited," Maggie agreed placidly. "She's gonna show me some new pictures her dad helped her take and we're going to put them in an album. She wants my *oh-pin-yun*."

"You do have excellent taste," Claire said. "I'm going to really need your opinion when we go shopping for a Christmas tree tonight."

Those words motivated Maggie to quickly finish her cereal, regardless of the potential impact on her tummy. "We both have busy days," she said. "But that will make them go fast until we get our tree."

Claire was glad that her astute daughter hadn't noticed or at least hadn't commented on her not eating anything herself for breakfast. Her stomach had its own jumble going on and didn't need any help from food, hastily consumed or otherwise.

She had always been a person who tried to take life as it came, who tried to be grateful for any opportunities that came her way, while also never letting her expectations get too high.

She had left as much of that high-school girl behind as

she could, but still carried small, hurt parts of her like the pieces of a lonely child's broken toy.

Now, though, she couldn't help herself from having expectations. She wanted this to work out. She wasn't at all sure what her next step was going to be if it didn't.

Sam will be there. I don't have to do this alone.

When Claire arrived at Town Hall, her eyes instinctively sought out Sam. She didn't see him, but she wasn't immediately concerned.

She saw Grace and Shirley, though, deep in conversation. When they saw her, they waved her over.

"You're presenting third on the agenda," Grace said.

Claire would have preferred to have gone first, a nerve-racking prospect by its own right, but at least it would be over with. On the other hand, going third meant that Sam would have time to get there if there was something holding him up.

He's going to be here.

"Okay, thanks," Claire said. "And thank you again for letting Maggie land in on John and Gloria this morning."

"Don't thank me," Grace said. "I'm just hanging out with some interesting people at a meeting, drinking some truly mediocre coffee."

They laughed and Claire was grateful as some of the tension eased out of her body.

Soon, Mayor Stephanie Barclay's assistant was beckoning them into the meeting room.

How many times had she sat across from Sam at this table? Claire wondered. How many times had she listened to his calm voice, sounding so sure of what was right, of what was needed, while she was the one who tended to get more riled defending her vision?

Now she knew more about him than she'd ever anticipated and she knew the torments he hid behind that calm facade.

She took a chair between Shirley and Grace, and as troubled curiosity regarding Sam's whereabouts threatened to flare into anxiety, she took deep breaths, inhaling and exhaling.

"Hey..." Grace nudged her softly. "It's going to be fine. You'll do a great job, I know it."

If she also thought it odd that Sam wasn't there yet, she wasn't saying so.

She probably doesn't want to add to my nerves.

She smiled weakly in Grace's direction.

The meeting was called to order and Claire tried not to look in the direction of the door, but did her best to concentrate on what was being said.

The topic was about getting a new play structure at the elementary school. From what she could remember, it hadn't been that long since a new structure had been erected, but one of the young mothers was a bit obsessive about following a supermom blogger and took all of the woman's suggestions to heart.

Claire considered pointing out that the play structure the school had was only a few years old, but she didn't have the wits to gather her thoughts.

How am I supposed to present if I can't even pull it together enough to comment?

The others in the room reflected her thoughts, though, voting against the new structure.

The second agenda item was announced and there was still no sign of Sam.

Claire's nervous hand reached toward the water pitcher. Shirley noticed and intervened, pouring her a glass with a sympathetic smile.

Claire tried not to guzzle the water, savoring the coldness against her tight throat.

No doubt, Shirley and Grace thought she was just nervous about the presentation, which she was, especially because as the minutes ticked by, it increasingly looked like she would be doing it on her own.

They were right to a certain degree if that was what they were thinking, because this was not a one-person presentation. They had agreed that Sam would address the financial aspects and budgetary concerns, allowing Claire to shine at what she did best—expressing creative potential inherent in a community garden.

Of course, as a business owner, she dealt with the budget side of things out of necessity, but it was far from her favorite part of running the shop and she regularly relied on her financial adviser to keep her up to speed.

She'd believed that, together, she and Sam would make the perfect presentation.

But he hadn't shown up and now, behind her worry and frustration, a fear that something had happened to him started to creep through her on spidery little feet.

But the greatest fear of all was that he had changed his mind and had decided that he didn't support her after all.

She took another swallow of water and blinked to focus her swimming eyes on the discussion between the secondhand-bookstore owner, who wanted to set up a coffee corner in his store, and the owner of the café, who wondered why people would need to go to a bookstore for coffee, when there was already perfectly good coffee to be had at her place, not to mention at Murphy's Restaurant.

The discussion went in circles for several minutes until it was finally agreed that they would table it until after Christmas.

Claire was considering how she might be able to manage slipping out to try to phone Sam, not at all sure what she would say if she managed to reach him, when she heard Mayor Barclay as she announced, "Okay, next up we have… Oh, isn't this interesting?" Her eyebrows rose slightly as her mouth quirked with amusement. "Pastor Sam Meyer and Claire Casey presenting *together*—" she put a slight emphasis on the word "—on how using the property beside Love Blooms for a community garden could benefit all." She sat back and folded her hands. "Well, this I am looking forward to."

"Uh, Sam isn't here," Claire said as she stood, "so I guess it's just me."

She was unable to take any pleasure from the mayor's reaction to the idea of her and Sam presenting together, even though it was exactly what she'd anticipated.

She was outgoing in her store, she was fully capable of expressing her opinions in a group setting, but this was something completely different.

She had never done a formal presentation with all eyes upon her, never mind while fighting the poisonous mix of worry and anger over Sam not showing up.

In all the ways she had imagined today turning out, she had never even considered that he wouldn't be here, as he'd promised to be, which made the current circumstances even more hurtful.

It was like she was hearing her own voice through a distant fog when she presented. She was surprised that her legs didn't collapse under her.

If she'd known the task was going to fall to her, she would have been better prepared to speak on the financial side of things. But this only went to prove, Claire thought as she still tried to continue with a coherent presentation, that it really didn't do any good to count on anyone but yourself.

The inadequacy she felt over being ill-prepared spilled over into the part of the presentation that she had been looking forward to giving and she wound things up more quickly than she'd intended, not making eye contact with anyone as she returned to her seat.

"Thank you, Claire," Mayor Barclay said after a brief pause. "I believe this has the beginnings of a good idea, but I think we need more detail before we can come to any kind of decision."

It was all so humiliating and Claire couldn't wait to get out of there and gather herself before she had to retrieve Maggie.

"You did just fine," Grace whispered when Claire sat down again, but her expression was one of a person offering sympathy, not praise.

"No, I didn't." She was too weary to put on a happy face and didn't bother to make herself pay attention to the last couple of agenda items. Her heart and mind were racing too fast for that even if she'd been inclined to.

"I'm sure Sam has a good explanation," Shirley said in a lowered tone. "It's not like him to simply not show up. Everything's going to be fine, Claire."

Claire wanted to believe that, but it was getting harder by the second.

It wasn't only hard to believe that the community garden would work out—it was hard to believe she'd actually let herself imagine that she wouldn't be alone.

By praying in the wordless, incoherent groans that the Holy Spirit promised to understand, Sam finally managed to get himself out of bed and to the small private chapel at

Good Shepherd Church. It was a space that was used for both joyful occasions like small, intimate weddings and for tragic ones, like those funerals people never expected to be attending.

Now it was a haven for Sam, not that it stopped the torment in his brain, but it was a place that could remind him of what he clung to by sheer discipline, study and persistent reminders that God's Word was what was true, not the clatter in his head.

He sat in the quiet emptiness listening to his own breathing, smelling the cedar wood of the pews and the wax of candles. After what seemed like a very long time, the beast retreated slightly. It wasn't fully back in its cave—that was too much to hope for—but other thoughts were making their way forward.

Claire.

Sam sank his head down into his hands. This was anguish separate from the muddled blackness. This was sharp and real, and cut deep.

What must she be thinking of me, Lord?

Yet, even as he asked himself the question, he knew he was far from being able to approach her and explain himself.

I should have stayed away. I knew I wasn't going to be any good to anyone over the long term and now I've proved it.

He had the sudden sensation of no longer being alone and turned his head to find Ann standing in the doorway.

"Pastor," she said. Then, when he didn't reply, she asked, "You're back from the town-council meeting?"

"I didn't go."

Ann didn't comment or ask what in the world, when the

council meeting—and Claire Casey—was probably all he'd talked about for the past week or so.

Instead, she slid into the pew beside him and for a few minutes they sat together, looking at the cross, the symbol of their salvation, on the front wall of the chapel.

"I wasn't there for her, Ann," Sam finally said, still looking straight ahead. "I promised her I would be and I didn't follow through."

"That's not like you, Pastor," Ann said. He could feel her gaze on him then, until he turned his head and met her eyes.

"I don't just mean that I never expected you to do something like that," she said. "I mean that what you did is *not* you. It's something that happened, something that got under your skin, which maybe someday you'll want to tell me about, and you've got to know that I won't judge you. But whatever it is, it's not who you are and it doesn't have to define you."

Sam nodded, acknowledging her words, trying to process them.

They lapsed into silence again. Sam continued to think and pray, pushing back against the darkness.

He'd told one person. Was that only the beginning? Could he tell Ann, and after that another person and yet another?

His depression would always be part of him, but if he kept shedding light on it instead of trying to hide it, if he sought the counseling he would have encouraged anyone else in his position to seek, maybe it would lose some of its power.

"I suffer from depression, Ann," Sam said. "I had an episode this morning, one of the worst ones I've had in quite some time, and I couldn't make it to the meeting. I can't imagine what Claire must have thought."

Ann looped her arm through his. "She probably wondered why," she agreed. "Knowing Claire, she was probably equal parts upset with you and worried about you. But you'll talk to her when you're ready and you'll iron it out."

Sam shook his head. "Claire hasn't been able to count on people," he said, not willing to go into any details about her personal life, but, then again, Ann probably had some idea. "It took some convincing for her to let me be on her side and now I've blown it. I doubt she wants to hear anything I have to say."

"I doubt that's true," Ann said. "Give her a chance, give yourself another chance. You both deserve it." Ann paused and then said, "Pastor?"

He waited.

"Thank you for telling me about your depression. I only wish you'd done it a long time ago so you'd know that you're not alone."

Ann left him then and he remained sitting in the chapel for a long time afterward.

He still wasn't sure if he deserved a second chance, but Claire certainly deserved an apology.

If only he could gather the strength and courage to offer one.

Chapter Thirteen

For the next few days, Claire went through the motions.

Christmas was only days away, and while she usually loved the season and everything it stood for, this year it was scarred with disappointment and more questions than answers.

But she feigned enjoyment for Maggie's sake, and Rachel's, as they put up the tree, got their favorite Christmas goodies and watched the seasonal specials on television.

Every day, she opened Love Blooms, put on a smile for the customers and even made a few sales.

One morning, Dorothy and Patrice Larsen came in and browsed while Dorothy asked questions and made complimentary comments about the flowers. Patrice hovered, stealing shy glances at Claire, and looked like she wanted to say something. She was pale and jittery but Claire told herself it was pre-wedding nerves. After all, January was drawing closer all the time.

A strange idea simmered within her that they had changed their minds about the flowers but were afraid to say so. But, no, that was ridiculous. She couldn't imagine Dorothy Larsen ever being afraid to ask for what she wanted.

On the way home, though, Claire couldn't help wondering what she would say if they really had changed their minds and wanted her to do the flowers. Would she let pride and hurt feelings propel her to say that she was too busy to take them on, or would she acknowledge that she needed the business and was grateful to have it?

But even as these responses played tug-of-war, she was already imagining how she would manage her schedule if she was called to pull something together in the time that remained before the wedding.

She didn't really believe that it was something she was going to have to concern herself with, but these days she was latching on to anything that gave her something to think about other than Sam.

He still hadn't reached out, and after seeing him in church on Sunday from a distance—he had led the prayers of the community and had disappeared before church emptied— something in her had hardened.

Yes, she knew that he suffered from depression, but if he could pull himself together enough to perform his duties, why couldn't he find it in himself to give her some kind of explanation for breaking his promise?

She reminded herself that she had lived her whole life without Sam Meyer as part of it and she could certainly continue to do so. The heartache that tore her away from sleep at night was a persistent reminder that it was best not to need someone.

On the day before Christmas Eve, Dorothy and Patrice paid another visit to Love Blooms, but this time Dorothy was clearly on a mission. Instead of browsing, or pretending to browse, she headed straight in Claire's direction, Patrice trailing in her wake.

Claire kept an eye on the other customers in the shop. She wouldn't neglect them for Dorothy. She didn't owe her any favors.

But then she prayed silently for a better attitude. *Lord,*

*please help me listen with an open mind to whatever they
have to say.*

"Hello, Claire." Dorothy spoke in her usual firm, well-modulated voice but, somehow, there was a hint of vulnerability underneath. "We would appreciate just a moment of your time."

"Of course," Claire said. "How can I help you?"

"We want you to do my flowers," Patrice blurted.

Claire could see that Dorothy had wanted more time to ease into the request but then she simply nodded.

"Yes, after considering our options, we've realized that you really did want to create something memorable for Patrice's wedding and that we perhaps could have given you more freedom to do that."

Okay, it wasn't exactly an apology, but Claire realized it was about as close as she was going to get.

"I would really love to help you out," she said cautiously. "I mean, it would still be an honor to do the flowers for the wedding, but if I'm being honest, you haven't given me a lot of time to work with. It's almost Christmas and I don't plan on doing anything other than appreciating a few days off with Maggie. Before we know it, it will be New Year's and your wedding not long after."

"Are you saying no?" Dorothy asked. "If it's a question of money, I'd be more than willing to pay whatever you ask."

"It's not a question of money," Claire said, even while she inwardly acknowledged that extra money would certainly help, especially not knowing if the community garden was ever going to happen after she botched the proposal. "Like I said, it's a question of time and what I want my priorities to be. Can I please have until the day after Christmas to think about it?"

Patrice's hopeful face collapsed slightly and Dorothy

went thin-lipped, but she said, "Of course. I suppose we owe you that much at least."

"If you do decide to do the flowers, and I hope you do," Patrice said, "I'm sure that Sam would do whatever he could to help you."

Sam. Hearing his name spoken by another slammed into Claire's gut, almost taking her breath away.

"I don't think so. I'm not really in touch with Sam these days," she said, marveling at her own composure, as the taste of his name in her mouth was something she wished she could savor but was bitter instead. "We haven't spoken in a little while and I don't expect that to change."

"Don't be so sure about that," Dorothy said. Her face didn't exactly soften—it never did—but her eyes showed a kindness and understanding Claire had not expected.

"We talked to him a couple of days ago," she explained. "He said he'd wronged you and is trying to figure out a way to apologize. It was actually him that urged us to give you a chance to give *us* a second chance."

"He did?" Claire whispered through her clogging throat.

"Yes," Dorothy said, returning to her firm self. "I told him he should do the same for himself and give you a chance to forgive whatever it is he did. He also told us about some… struggles he's had over the years. I expect he will tell you all about it, if he hasn't already."

"He has," Claire said.

So Sam had told the Larsens the truth about his depression. He was opening up about it, not hiding it anymore.

It was the bravest thing she had ever heard.

She could be brave, too. She could be forgiving, which was a bravery in itself, and she could ask God for forgiveness for letting her pride and anger color how she had judged Sam and for letting it get in the way of a reopened door.

"I've changed my mind," Claire said. "I don't need to think about it. Patrice…" She paused, but at the young woman's hopeful expression, she was sure in her heart that she was doing the right thing. "It would be my pleasure to do the flowers for your wedding."

When her satisfied customers left and a few more trickled into the shop looking for last-minute things, Claire told herself to enjoy the rest of the day and the days ahead celebrating the birth of the Lord.

If God could bring the birth of the savior into a humble stable, He could surely help her figure out how she would get the arrangements done in time.

He could help her find the courage to be the one to reach out to Sam first.

As she worked, she thought about what a good listener he was, how he was respectful even when he disagreed with her and how he encouraged her to be herself, praised her creativity, helped her to believe—maybe without even knowing he was doing it—that she was beautiful.

And she realized that, more than anything, she needed to tell him that she loved him.

On Christmas Eve, Sam watched people pour into the church, filling the pews. There were many regulars, as well as the ones he expected to see only on special occasions. But they all had a place and they all played their part.

He had officially turned down a job offer that morning. It seemed odd to him now that he had believed for so long that a new setting was the best way to escape what plagued him. No, there was much work to be done here and, besides, his depression had to be faced head-on no matter where he was.

When he saw Claire, with an excited Maggie clinging

to her hand, and Rachel slip into a pew near the back of the church, he prayed that he would have an opportunity to talk to her before they left following the service. Usually, people liked to linger after services to visit and indulge in the simple refreshments offered, but on Christmas Eve, they were understandably eager to get on with their own celebrations.

It might surprise people to know that, as he looked out on the congregation on Christmas Eve, he saw as many sad, or at least pensive, faces as ones filled with joy and anticipation.

But, then again, maybe it wouldn't surprise them at all.

He was beginning to realize that the more open he was about his depression, the more willing people were to honor his humanness, with all of its flaws, and to share theirs in return.

The service passed with the old but ever new readings and carols. Candles were lit as all joined in singing "Silent Night," the peace was shared and Christmas greetings exchanged, and the service came to a close.

Sam hurried to station himself at the exit that Claire would be using based on where she'd sat. He greeted each person who passed by, making eye contact and warmly pressing their hands, but his heart danced and his mind filled with all the things he needed to say to Claire.

When he saw her, next in line to be greeted, their eyes met and it was like a brightly colored reel played through his head of all the moments he had been aware of her: her passion, her stubbornness, her determination, her creativity, her courage…

I love her.

There were only a few people left behind her, so he

squeezed her hand and asked in a low tone, "Will you please wait for me? It won't take long but I need to talk to you."

Claire bit her lip and glanced in Rachel's direction.

Rachel nodded, reading the situation. "I'll take Maggie to get a candy cane. I see Ann is handing them out."

As soon as he was able, Sam ushered Claire into the small chapel, thinking of how shattered he had been the last time he sat in there.

But he hadn't been alone. God was there and God had made sure that Sam knew that other people were there for him, too.

Now was the time, though, to try to explain why he hadn't been there for Claire.

"Please sit," he said and gestured. Claire did so, and he sat beside her, almost at the same time. Then they angled their bodies to face each other.

"Claire," Sam began, "the day of the town-council meeting… I don't even know if I can put into words what happened to me that morning, but I'm so sorry for not showing up. I can't tell you how sorry I am."

He took a deep breath. "I've told you about my depression, but it's so difficult to really explain to anyone exactly how or when it can hit hard, especially when I can't even explain it to myself."

"I'm sorry that I let myself think the worst of you," Claire said. "You trusted me about your depression, but instead of being understanding when the chips were down and knowing you must be going through something, I let old wounds get in the way. Please forgive me."

Sam swallowed and blinked away sudden tears. He had come to ask forgiveness and had not expected that Claire might also need it.

"I forgive you," he said. "Of course I do, not that I think there's anything to forgive."

"There's nothing for me to forgive you for, either," Claire said. "But I will say that I do if that helps us move past this."

Sam took her hand and they studied each other's faces.

"I want to move past this," Sam said. "I don't want to leave Living Skies. I especially don't want to leave you. I pray we share a future together, whatever life brings. But, Claire, this illness I struggle with. It's never going to just disappear. It's always going to be part of our lives."

"I know that," Claire said. "There are things that I bring with me, too, things that make me less than the person I know God wants me to be, the person I want to be for you. I still let old hurts and insecurities define who I am sometimes and I am striving not to do that."

"I know you are," Sam said, an emotional orchestra playing in every word he said. "We've both made mistakes, we both have imperfections and struggles, but I know we can help each other with that and I know that I love you."

For a moment the shy, lonely girl she had been shone out from Claire's eyes.

"You love me?" she whispered.

He nodded and raised her hand to his mouth, bestowing a kiss on it.

Then his beautiful, vivacious Claire was back, smiling widely, with the answer shining from her eyes before she even said it.

"I love you, too," she said.

Sam silently breathed a prayer that was filled with such gratitude he could hardly contain it.

The scripture from Ecclesiastes about the cord of three strands to him. He felt sure it was God telling him that if they waited to be perfect, they would never take a chance on a relationship. But if they kept God at the center of things, they could trust that it was worth taking a chance on a relationship.

* * *

On a beautiful Saturday afternoon in January, Sam sat beside Claire in Good Shepherd Church waiting for the wedding of Patrice Larsen to begin.

Before the ceremony started, Shirley Allen stopped by to tell them that council had approved the community garden. Sam and Claire had been unable to attend that meeting, but together, they had lifted the results to the Lord, deciding to trust whatever the outcome was.

Sam knew the bride was supposed to be the center of attention, but he wasn't at all sure that he'd be able to take his eyes off the woman dressed in deep emerald beside him.

He leaned over and whispered, "Do you remember our first kiss?"

Claire blushed beautifully. "Um…yes."

"Keep thinking about that," he whispered. "And of all the kisses to come. I have something I want to ask you tonight."

Later that day, Rachel had taken Maggie out for hot chocolate and Sam sat beside Claire on the love seat in her living room.

Holding both of Claire's hands to his heart, he said, "Claire, I want to spend all of my days working to be the best version of myself for you. I want to help you become the best version of yourself, not because I need you to change, but because I want you to be as happy with yourself as you want and deserve to be. I want us to share joys together, to face challenges and sorrows together. I want us to promise before God and our friends that we will always be there for each other. I want to share every moment of life with you. Claire Casey, will you marry me?"

"Yes," Claire answered, her whole heart in one word. "Yes, Sam, I will."

Epilogue

"Love Blooms was so busy all summer," Rachel mused gently as she fluffed out Claire's midlength veil, "you didn't get to be a June bride yourself."

"No, I'm a winter bride," Claire said with deep gratitude. Her eyes shone back at her from the mirror on the vanity table in her bedroom, while Rachel adjusted the tiara she wore.

She could still hardly believe she was having the princess wedding she had always secretly dreamed of.

She stood up and enveloped her sister in a hug. Rachel looked lovely in a sea-foam-green dress.

Across the room, Grace adjusted the sea-foam-green sash on flower girl Maggie's lacy white dress and then did the same for Gloria, who was their junior bridesmaid.

Claire gently smoothed down her ivory satin-and-lace wedding dress. She picked up the bouquet she had made herself to express all this day meant to her. The blue irises expressed faith, the yellow daffodils hope and the red lilies love.

She knew she would have all of these in her marriage to Sam.

A joy almost too large to contain bubbled up in Claire.

"Let's get to the church," she said. "I can't wait to see my groom."

Today, they would move forward together to share a life of faith, hope and, the greatest of all these, love.

* * * * *

Dear Reader,

Thank you so much for reading Sam and Claire's story. It means the world to me.

These characters fear that they will not be loved and accepted for who they are. I think that is a fear we can all identify with.

But, as they learn to trust each other, they find each other to be an unexpected source of encouragement. They also both turn to our Heavenly Father, knowing He is the source of all comfort.

We, too, can turn to God about anything at any time, remembering that in His eyes we are beautiful, valuable and always worthy of love.

I pray that this story blesses you.

Thank you for being such great readers!

Please email me at deelynn1000@hotmail.com and say hello if you enjoyed this story. You can also find me on Facebook at Donna Gartshore's Author Updates and on Instagram @dlgwrites.

Love,
Donna